AJA & SANTANA

A Dope Love Story

TINA B. & ANAK

MYSS SHAN

Aja & Santana

SUBSCRIBE

Text Shan to 22828 to stay up to date with new releases, sneak peeks, contest, and more....

SUBMISSIONS

To submit your manuscript to Shan Presents, please send the
first three chapters and synopsis to
submissions@shanpresents.com

Chapter One

AJA

May 30th, 2018

"Come on, girl. I don't know why you even let stupid ass Miles get to you! You look bomb as fuck!" My bitch Skylar complimented me as we sat on the back of her F-150 Truck. I sighed and kept glancing at the bench Miles and his niggas occupied.

"Yes friend, you look good! Fuck what that nigga say!" Braylon added.

I was self-conscious about everything. I made sure my braids was still in place and grabbed my phone so that I could stand up. I looked up and my eyes connected with Mack and he shook his head "no" so I sat right back down. Bray and Sky groaned and stood up.

"We be back then. We are going to get us something to drink and eat. If you want a plate get yo ass up and come get it g!" Skylar said, and they both walked off, leaving me to my miserable thoughts.

No matter how much I tried to gain confidence about my newfound weight gain, that confidence was shot the hell down. Going from a size five to a size sixteen was a drastic change in my weight. That's why I stayed at the gym every night no matter how tired I was. I sighed and ran my hand down my thighs. I was only eighteen years old, but my body felt like I was eighty. My small pudge was noticeable when I sat down, but when I stood up, you couldn't even tell it was there. I knew it was there, though, and Miles knew also. He reminded me every day how fat or sloppy I was. I admit I was a double cheeseburger, small fry, and iced tea away from being a full figure BBW but sloppy NEVER.

I wore a size sixteen in pants because my hips, thighs, and butt had grown tremendously with giving birth to my son four months ago. I wore a large in shirts but could easily pull off a crop top if I was confident enough like today. My face was round and my skin was the prettiest shade of peanut butter, with no blemishes, marks, or nothing on my face. My lips set big and pink, while my nose was small and kind of like a piggy. I'd grown to love my Ms. Piggy though. My eyes was a light hazel, and I was about ten in the face. My hair came to my shoulders, but I kept it in braids or either a sew-in. It really depends on if I could find some cheap but great quality weave. I was transitioning into the natural wave so wearing my real hair right now was totally out of the question.

"What you doing all alone?" Jason, the neighborhood CD man, asked. I looked around and everybody was mingling. At the beginning of every summer, the radio station and Indianapolis Public Schools would throw a block party and nonetheless here we all were. Instead of Indianapolis Public Schools throwing it this year, the hood came out and threw one. So if you were anybody, or shit a nobody, you were at the block party. Y'all know how the hood do, so you know it was lit! It was kids running around getting into trouble. It was women half naked walking back and forth trying to catch the eyes of the local drug dealers that was posted out here.

"I'm minding my business. What you want Jason? Why

you even stop to talk to me? You know how that nigga get when he drunk." I spoke lowly.

"Girl ain't nobody scared of that nigga but you! To you he crazy but to everybody else he a bitch!" Jason stupid ass said which instantly pissed me off.

"Go head on J!" I waved him off.

I wanted no parts of the foolery he was spitting. I knew it wouldn't end well with me if Miles saw Jason talking to me. After he kept talking and me ignoring him he finally got the hint and took off walking. I glanced at my phone and smiled at my screen saver. My baby boy Ashton was my everything. Miles Ashton White, Jr. was his name but I hated the name Miles so I called him MJ or Ashton. Ashton looked just like me with a head full of curly hair that I kept braided to the back. Only thing Aston got from his ugly ass daddy was the dimples. He was my complexion and had my lips, eyes, nose and all that; he even laughed and smiled like me. My baby was everything and more. I wouldn't trade his little chunky self for nothing in this world. Having my son put me in such a different head space! I was so tired of the bullshit with Miles it was crazy. Since I got pregnant this where all the weight gain came from and Miles stressing me out wasn't no help either.

I groaned and stood up when I saw a bitch stand in between Miles' legs. She had a body like Buffy but when she turned around she had a face only her mother could love. She was a little darker than me and had a green bob in her hair. What threw me off was the piercings lined her cheeks where I'm guessing dimples was supposed to be but it wasn't. Chick was ugly, no ifs, ands, or buts about it. She had a Squid-ward nose and her eyes was chink like. I don't know how to explain her but she wasn't hitting on shit. I started to walk towards them when she pushed his head back and he smacked her on the ass as she walked off.

"Wassup with that?" I asked once I made it to Miles and his homeboys.

He shrugged and shooed me away. I rolled my eyes and walked right back where I sat. He went right back to shooting dice like he had the money to lose. Yes, on top of me putting up with the verbal abuse, this nigga was flat out broke as fuck. All he had was the designer clothes my boosting ass cousin Yaya kept us laced with and the twenty-eighteen Challenger, that he skipped the payments on. Other than that, this nigga was broke, and I was taking care of his sorry ass. I was sick of his ass!

"You still sitting here?" Bray asked as she walked up. She had two plates in her hand and handed me one.

"Thanks friend but I don't even have an appetite." I said.

I was still bothered by the open disrespect Miles showed, and I was just ready to go get my son from my grandma and go home.

"Girl, you gone let that nigga stress you into a early grave!" Skylar shouted and we laughed.

"Shut up, bitch, yelling and shit... Yo, where is yo hearing aid at bitch?" I asked seriously.

"Girl, I dropped it in the toilet. I gotta go get another one." She smirked and started to eat again.

Chilling on the block the sun finally started to go down, and everybody that was sipping was drunk. Everybody's attention turned towards the bright orange Jaguar with high ass orange and silver rims that came speeding down the street. The music was bumping and blasting, and everybody in attendance of the block party was looking trying to see who was driving.

"That's my nigga, Tana. Aye Tana. Wassup Tana." I heard throughout the crowd.

I almost fainted when the windows rolled down and the nigga that was driving smiled showing off his bottom grill and pearly whites. It was like for a second our eyes connected and all we saw was each other until I felt my arm being snatched almost out of place. I snapped my head back getting ready to go off but quickly cowered when I turned to Miles with a death stare.

To the naked eye, it looked like a loving embrace how he was over me and holding my arm but the pain in my arm told otherwise.

"If you don't quit eye-fucking this nigga, I'mma break yo fucking face!" Miles gritted through a closed mouth and gripped my arm tighter.

"Matter of fact, rake yo hoe ass on and get my son and go home." He hissed and shoved me a little bit. When he let me go the tears that I was holding finally fell but I quickly wiped them. I stood up and started to fix my clothes. I was wearing some black high waist Victoria's Secret spandex with a black and white Victoria's Secret Loose fitting crop top with some black, silver, and white Victoria's Secret slides. I had on my matching Vicky fanny pack with light jewelry. My braids was pulled into a bun at the top leaving two single braids on the side.

"Aye?" I heard from behind. I kept looking at Miles to see when he was gone give me his keys to the car.

"Aye Mike?"

We both looked up and everybody was staring at us. The dude in the shiny car was calling Miles. Miles got overly geeked and started smiling. I knew dude was important because his car looked like it cost more than my whole life and the way he shut down the whole set let me know he was indeed the boss.

"Not you, her." he said shutting down Miles' whole ego. I looked up finally realizing he wanted my attention.

"Yeah you... Come here for a minute little momma." Tana said so cocky, and I looked at Miles for permission but also to see was he going to speak up about him wanting to talk to me.

Miles didn't take disrespect lightly especially when guys tried to get at me. I knew it was gone be some problems.

"Bitch go head. What the fuck you standing here looking stupid for?" Miles asked lowly enough for me to here.

He walked away and I turned to walk dude way, with shock plastered on my face. I knew it was going to be a problem when I get home tonight. Everybody else slowly turned around and started doing what they were doing. Minding they business.

"How you doing gorgeous?" Dude asked and stepped out of the car. The view of him from the inside of the car was nothing compared to him actually getting out of the car. This nigga has to be handpicked from Eve cause it had to be a sin to be this fine. I mean, he was fine fine. He stood over me, so I want to say about six feet six inches. He was dark-skinned with the smoothest skin ever to be a street nigga. His lips was full and juicy, and I just wanted to suck on them. He smiled as I took in his appearance. He screamed money. He was rocking a plain white Ralph Lauren polo shirt with some black Balmain pants, and on his feet was some white and black Gucci sneakers with the red bottoms. His hair was lined up to perfection and this nigga had waves so deep I was getting dizzy by looking at them. His jewelry was plain but he still rocked a watch and chain. This nigga was fine PERIOD!

"What's yo name sweetheart?" He asked and I shifted my weight to my other foot. For some reason I wasn't even self-conscious under his stare at all.

"I'm Aja ... You?" I asked. I don't even know why I was even asking. I'm pretty sure I wouldn't make it another day to see this nigga again.

"Santana. You got a man? Matter of fact, I don't give a fuck if you do. Let me take you out." Tana said and I laughed.

"You see that nigga right there?" I asked pointing back at Miles who was staring at us.

"That's my nigga. Been with him since I was fourteen. I'm now nineteen. That's disrespect......" I started but he laughed and got back into his car.

"Nah ma... What's disrespectful is that nigga let me get at you while he right there. He didn't say anything or stop you. Check this. You lost your chance on getting my number with that smart ass mouth." Santana said and pulled off. When I turned around smiling I was met with a fist straight to the face. I must've forgot to say he wasn't only mental abusive, and broke. He was physically abusive also.

Chapter Two

SANTANA

I drove away from chick cracking up laughing. I was a arrogant ass nigga but I couldn't even help myself. I was a handsome little killer and any female I wanted I could have. So when I pulled up to the block party my brother and I sponsored and saw shorty I was captivated by her presence. Like amazed by her. No other female ever caught my eye like shorty. She was with her weak ass nigga but I gave no fucks. He was a peon anyways. Wanted to be down with me and my brother for years. We ain't fuck with him cause he was lame. When her thick ass rejected me, it bruised my ego. Only for a little bit. She was thick as hell, man, and pretty as fuck. I knew she was loyal because she rejected me for her weak ass baby daddy.

Ring, ring, ring!

"What it do foo?" I asked my brother Montana.

"Shit, shit. Niggas told me yo hot ass went to that block party. You tripping dog." Montana voiced and I smacked my lips.

"Man, nigga who reporting back to you? I'mma grown ass nigga." I said and it was his turn to smack his lips.

"Bitch, I'm the oldest. So whatever I say go." Montana yelled and I laughed.

"Bro, you only the oldest by one minute. Chill with that." I said and we both laughed.

"Where you at? I'm at the spot!" he said, and I hung up as I pulled up to our main spot.

When I stepped out the car, it was niggas posted and stings parlaying around the trap. I shook my head because I hated when my brother wanted to meet at this hot ass spot. Yeah, this trap made us so much money on a daily, but this right here brought attention. I wasn't the smartest, but I knew this wasn't a good idea when niggas be snitching and the feds be watching. Everything in my body told me to turn the fuck around and go on about my merry way.

"Wassup Tana?" My little nigga C.J asked riding on his bike.

C.J. was our lookout. He was only twelve and came to me a few months ago talking about he wanted to get down with us. He saw how we made money on the block he lived on, and his momma was struggling. C.J. intentionally wanted to start hustling on the block, but my conscious wouldn't let me do that to the young bull, so he has been my lookout every since. He rode his bike up and down the block all day so before anything could pop off he was peeping first and reporting straight to me. For that, I paid him faithfully every chance I saw him.

"Yo C. How was your day?" I asked. I wanted him to lie and say anything other than he ain't go. It was my business to know any and everything about whoever worked for me, and when I rode up to his school yesterday they told me he hadn't been there.

"Man, Santana is not even..." He started to say but I shook my head.

"What I tell you dude ... Go to school and then hit the

block. If you can't do that I can't have you on my block my nigga." I told him and he sighed.

"I'm going to summer school." He boasted and I dabbed him up.

"That's my man... Look, I want you to go to my mom's center Monday, so she can hook you up with some shit." I told him and pulled out some cash from my pocket. I peeled off a few hundreds and gave it to him. "Gone head and take that home and come back and post up." I told him, and he smiled and rode off on his bike. As he rode off, Montana walked on the porch with six duffle bags, two in each hand and kicking two.

"We shutting this bitch down. These niggas don't know how to fucking act. Causing all this unwanted attention. Not getting ran up for none of these bitch ass niggas!" He snapped as the clean-up van pulled up.

"What happened in there?" I asked. If the Chinks was here then I know it was a body or few around.

"Had to get rid of a few niggas. Niggas done let they balls drop." Montana yelled, and I shook my head. I was shocked because Montana was the calm one. I was the trigger happy one. I guess he was fed up. He threw two bags my way, and I caught them.

"You gotta make the drop and take this to the Wash." Montana said and walked to my car. I hit the trunk of my key fob and he set the bags under the floorboard.

"Why can't you nigga?" I asked and he pointed to his motorcycle.

"Alright then, nigga, shut up." He added and dabbed me up.

"You coming to Unc grand opening tonight?" I asked and he smacked his lips.

"Of course, nigga. I don't fuck with that nigga, but if you going then I am to." He said and I nodded.

"Alright, meet me at my crib at eleven." I told him and hopped into my car.

Soon as l I pulled off, fire trucks and ambulances passed me going towards the neighborhood I just pulled away from. Being nosey, I hit a U-turn and followed. Down the block from our spot, it was yellow tape and police everywhere. I laughed when I saw Montana standing on his motorcycle looking too. I parked, made sure my strap was tucked, and hopped out.

"What's going on?" I asked Montana as he chatted with a few of his niggas I ain't really fuck with.

"Man, it's bad." Montana said, and I started to walk closer to get a better view. Peaking over the cop cars and yellow tape, I saw two people pushing a body bag out followed by somebody else pushing a body bag out. What came out of the house next shocked me the most. Two police escorting my little nigga C.J. out in handcuffs. He looked at me and tears filled his eyes. He mouthed "I'm sorry." Then they took him away.

Chapter Three

AJA

"Thank you for calling Nissan call center. Am I speaking to Mr. Young?" I asked as I answered my last call for the day. I sighed and yawned at the same time. I have been here since five-thirty this morning and it was going on seven o'clock at night.

"Yes, this Young. Look, I ordered an all-white twenty nineteen, Jeep Cherokee to be at a specific address in the morning. I told the Bit.... Look, I told the nigga that I talked to a few days ago I pay extra for short notice. He said it was cool, and they'd have it there by today! Now I'm telling you, if ma dukes don't have this car by today. That's on you." Mr. Young spat and I sighed.

"Sir, can I get your address? Where it's being delivered to." I asked, and he riddled off the address as I typed on my computer.

"Sir, are you at the address?" I asked and rolled my eyes.

"Yeah, it ain't here. Why you think I'm calling you." He said smartly.

"Okay, look outside!" I interrupted. After a second he hung up the phone.

Dummy.

I hung up and gathered all my stuff. Skylar and I met up at the break room after we both clocked out.

"I'm so tired of this damn job working with these disrespectful ass people." Skylar vented as I grabbed my stuff.

"Girl shit, me too! I can't wait until my nigga get on top so he can take care of me!" I said, and we looked at each other. We busted out laughing as we walked to Skylar's car. I hopped into the passenger and Sky hopped in the driver.

"How are you been feeling?" Sky asked. I pulled the sun visor down and looked at my face. The makeup did a great job hiding my black eye but knowing what was under the makeup is what hurts.

"I been okay. I just need two more pay checks then I'm out of there." I said, and we pulled up to Bray's job and she hopped straight in.

"Wassup y'all?" Bray spoke as she took off her two-piece jacket set. Sky and I spoke back.

"Anyways, all I need is two more checks then I'm done with his ass!" I repeated, and they both smacked they lips.

"I'm sorry friend, and I wouldn't be a real ass friend if I ain't say this. You said that the last time." Sky replied.

"The time before that... Oh yeah, then that time before that." Bray added in and Sky agreed.

"Okay, well shit... It's harder than what it seems. He watches Ashton while I work."

"That's all he do is baby sit his own damn son!" Bray yelled interrupting me.

"Babysit! Dassit! Who the hell asks a father to babysit they own child." Bray then added and quickly looked at me.

"Okay, well damn. I don't even wanna talk about it no-more!" I told them getting irritated.

These two bitches always made me the topic of the conversation. I knew my nigga wasn't shit, but that's the point... MY nigga, not there's! Miles was fucked up, but he hasn't always been like that. I knew Miles loved me! Shit we been thuggin since freshman year! Shit been rocky for us every since I graduated last year.

"Y'all kill me acting like y'all shit don't stink! I don't need to be reminded of something I already know." I told them, and Skylar smacked her lips.

"First of all, bitch, nobody said our shit don't stink, but bitch we give a fuck about you. We don't wanna see yo ass with another black eye or broken fucking bone. Excuse the fuck outta me, but if us telling you that we want better for you is getting on yo nerves, then go find friends that wanna see you get fucked up and laugh at yo ass!" Skylar said, and we both turned and looked at her. We all started laughing and Bray spoke up.

"We for real though sis. This shit ain't healthy. Shit since nobody wanna speak up about what the fuck happened last weekend I'mma say something... That shit was embarrassing and sad as fuck. Like I didn't know if you were gone be mad at us or what." Bray spoke out and I sighed.

"As long as y'all been around, how many times y'all done helped me when that nigga put his hands on me. I would never be mad at y'all. I was just mad cause, I mean, everybody know this nigga abusive as fuck, but damn, muthafuckas ain't have to see for they self. " I said and sighed.

After picking Ashton up from my grandma, we pulled up to my apartment building. I sighed and waved to my girls. I promised that I would meet them at Olive Garden tomorrow afternoon. I unlocked my door and heard laughter then talking. I was shocked because it wasn't Miles laughing; it was a female. I shut the door and put my purse down on the table. I lived in a two bedroom apartment in the middle of the projects. I have been working for this call center for about two years, and it was paying bills. Barely at that. Taking care of Ashton, Miles and bills I definitely didn't have extra money for myself. I wasn't tripping though. I did my own hair and lashes, Sky did my brows and make up when I wanted it done and Bray did nails. We hooked each other up. When I wanted new clothes then I would call my cousin Yaya she would hook me up in exchange for a free hair-do or so.

Stepping foot into the living room, I laid Ashton down on the couch. On the long couch was Miles and some chick. I didn't care that he hung with bitches. shit he was a bitch himself! I cared because they were too cozy with her feet in his lap. They were just laughing about some shit like I wasn't even standing there.

"Uhm." I coughed and kicked my shoes off. I was ready to beat her ass and the way I was feeling he could've got it too!

"Who is this?" I asked Miles mugging the chick.

"This Dej." He started to say but I interrupted him.

"I don't care who she really is. Why the fuck do she got her feet in yo lap and y'all just big chilling in this muthafucka!?" I hissed getting ready to pop off. She slowly raised her feet and started to laugh awkwardly.

"What's funny, Bitch? Did I tell a joke?" I asked shifting my weight to one side. Five...

I counted down.

"You funny... Look, I'mma go ahead and go. Call me if you come out later Mack." She said and got ready to hug him but before she could reach I grabbed her by her hair.

This bitch didn't know what to do. She started screaming instantly, which made Ashton cry and that's the only reason why I let the bitch hair go. Miles stood up and walked the bitch out and I laughed. I picked Ashton up and took him to my room and laid him in the swing. I put my son pacifier in his mouth and he drifted off to sleep.

Ashton was still in his prime so sleep and eat was all he knew. I couldn't wait until my baby get old enough so he could love on his mommy. I grabbed my robe and towel so I could shower. I don't understand why the hell he constantly disrespects me when I'm the only one ever been down for his bitch ass! Yeah, he was a punk. Everybody in the hood know how that nigga be getting stood on. I'm the only one scared of his ass like Jason said.

I stepped out of my clothes and under the hot water. I let the water run down my whole body, even my hair. I had to take my hair down cause Miles pulled out a handful of my braids, so lately I been rocking an iron out middle part to cover my edges. My cousin YaYa texted me earlier and told me she got hands on some good ass wavy bundles and would give me three and a closure if I did her a bob, so she was on her way over in a few.

I heard Miles come in the bathroom talking to himself and then he left out. After about thirty-five minutes I got out and dried my body off. I slipped on my robe and went to my room. Miles wasn't nowhere to be found, and I thanked God that his ass left. I wasn't fucking with him, and after stripping my covers and sheets off my bed I dressed it with fresh sheets from the closet. I slipped on some black lace panties and a matching bra from Torrid the plus size store. I slipped on some black Victoria's Secret leggings with the pink Victoria secret band on it. Then slipped on a matching black and pink Vicky shirt. I put my Victoria's Secret slides on and grabbed my baby monitor. My apartment wasn't that big but with the door shut I couldn't hear if he cried or not. After cleaning up my apartment and turning some music on I set my hair station up in my sitting room and started dinner. I was cooking some baked salmon, broccoli and rice. I was trying this diet with no fried foods, no bread, pop, chips, candy, of course, and more stuff that didn't matter because I didn't really care for it anyways.

Ring, ring, ring.

I rolled my eyes at the incoming call and pressed talk then speaker.

"Correctional industrial complex. To accept this call, press zero. To refuse this call, hang up or press one to prevent calls," I pressed zero then waited until the voice came through.

"Bout time you answered the phone. What, you ignoring yo momma now?" My mother Asia asked. Yes my mother's name is Asia. Please don't even ask why my name is Aja too. My momma just spelled my name different because that's just what fucked up people do!

"No ma, I wasn't ignoring you. I just have a life." I vented and sat down at the table.

"Girl, don't get smart with me. How my grand-boy?" Asia asked and I smiled.

"He's doing good ma. He's getting chunky as hell." I smiled thinking about my son.

"I bet he is. How are you?" She asked and I sighed.

"I'm okay. Working... I'm getting ready to do Yaya hair right now." I told her and she laughed.

"I have been hearing about that damn girl in this damn place. Tell her ass stay out them White people stores for her ass be here with me." My momma stressed. "You wanna know what else I been hearing in here?" She asked.

"No, but I bet you gone tell me anyways!" I said opening the door up for Yaya as she knocked.

"Yeah you gone listen muthafucka! I heard that weak pussy baby daddy of yours been out there beating yo ass! Now, I'mma tell you this like I told Nae-Nae when she came in here rapping telling everybody. Don't be letting that big punk ass nigga put his fucking hands on you! If I find out

I'mma have Pat and Stink come over there and fuck his ass up. He must not know."

"Thank you for using GTL goodbye." The automatic voicemail came over the phone and hung up. I laughed and sat my phone down. I don't know why my crazy ass momma even called with that bullshit. She know them people gone cut the phone off soon as her ass started talking crazy!

"What Aunty A want?" Yaya said pulling clothes, weave, shoes, phones, and even jewelry out the two garbage bags she brought with her.

"Damn cuz, you fucked em up." I told her ignoring the questions she asked. I finished cooking and made our plates to eat, while she sat down on the floor sorting her stuff out.

"You know it. You know I had to bring my fave something first. I hooked my godson up too!" Yaya twerked while sitting down. She pulled out some baby clothes and baby shoes. I smiled and hugged her.

"That's my girl." I told her as she handed me some stuff.

"See if you can fit that." Yaya said and I quickly hopped up trying everything on she passed me. If I couldn't fit it, I was squeezing my tiny ass up in it.

The next morning I woke up and the first thing I did was make Ashton a bottle. Today was my only day off so I was up bright and early. I needed to get out and pay some bills and handle everything I needed. Ashton was still knocked out, not budging. I put him in his baby rocker in the bathroom as I brushed my teeth and got in the shower. After showering for about fifteen minutes, I jumped out and dried off. Wrapping the towel around my body, I applied a little bit of makeup and took my scarf off. The thirty-inch weave I was rocking was wet and wavy, and my closure was nailed by yours truly. Muah.

I made sure my baby hair was intact and on fleek then I grabbed my son and washed him off. After I lotioned and powdered myself and my son down, I slipped him on a white under onesie then slipped him on a one piece grey and white Nike jumpsuit. I made sure his little gold bracelet and necklace was on courtesy of his god momma. I slipped his grey, white and black Air Max on his feet and slipped on my panties. I slipped on a white fitted Maxi dress that was strapless and fitted down to my ankles.

On my feet was some white Nike slides that Skylar had blinged out for me. Looking myself over I grabbed my blue jean jacket and put Ashton in his car seat. Putting on my silver hoops, I grabbed my purse and went to my closet. Going all through my closet, I grabbed the shoe box and emptied the money out in my purse. Gathering my son's diaper bag, I ordered my Uber and headed out. First stop was my bank to deposit the money and then the next stop was Olive Garden with my girls.

BRAYLON

"Girl, I been craving this salad." I said as we waited for Aja to arrive. We all decided to meet at Olive Garden today for some much needed girl time.

"Okay, me too! Talked to aunty?" Skylar asked me but I shook my head no.

"Nope, she hasn't called me in a few weeks." I replied back as Aja came rushing through the door.

"Sorry, I'm late. I had to stop at the bank." She said and sat Ashton down in the booster chair.

"You good. You look pretty." I complimented her and she smiled.

"Thank you. I don't feel cute. I feel fat!" She sighed and reached for the bread sticks to give it to Ash.

"You are fat but you are pretty!" Skylar said and I nodded.

"Hey I'm Tasha. I'm the waitress. What can I get you to drink. " our waitress asked Aja.

"I'll have a water." She responded and the waitress walked away.

"Who the hell is he? Why he keep looking over here?" Skylar said making Aja and I look around then look back.

"That's him." Aja blushed and ducked a little.

"That's Santana?" I said.

"That is him!" Skylar said and laughed.

"He keep looking at you Aja!" I told her and she blushed. Then, she looked around the restaurant like somebody was watching her.

"Girl, that nigga is not here!" I said rolling my eyes.

"Shut up!" Aja said and sighed.

"I can't help it!" She said lowly.

"Get the fuck away from his ass!" Skylar said and I nodded.

"Yeah, please do! I don't wanna have to kill that nigga if he put his hands on you again!" I told her truthfully and she smiled.

"I love y'all." she told us and her phone started ringing.

"Hello?" Aja answered.

"Correctional industrial complex. To accept this call, press zero. To refuse this call, hang up or press one to prevent calls." She presses one then my aunty Asia voice came through the speaker.

"Hey Ma." Aja said.

"Hey baby. What are you doing?" She asked.

"I'm at lunch with Bray and Sky. Say hi, I have you on speaker." Aja said and we all said hi.

"Hey daughters. How have y'all been? Y'all taking care of my baby?" Asia asked and I smiled.

"You know we is aunty. How are you? You get the money I sent you?" I asked.

"Yes I did niece. I been good, staying on yo momma ass! She been in lock down since last week. I meant to call you and tell you but I lost yo number." Asia said and I got sad. I missed my mother deeply and other than Aja and Sky she was my best friend for real.

"I'mma write her then. I was wondering why she wasn't calling me." I said and Asia sighed.

"Yeah, her ass done fucked up! And......"

"Thank you for using GTL, good-bye." The phone said and I sighed.

"I don't know why she use that language over these people's phone. They don't play that shit." Aja said and the waitress came back with her water.

"We ready to order now." I told her. She pulled out her notebook and we all ordered our food.

The whole time at lunch I kept seeing Aja sneak glances at Santana's table. I laughed to myself because she swears she wasn't interested in him though.

After lunch we headed back to my crib where we just chilled out until Aja had to get home.

MONTANA

"All this money we make and you want this?" Santana asked and I laughed.

I was high as hell off the best weed in the city. My shit.

This nigga was so arrogant it made me think he was light skinned. NOO, this nigga was black as hell. I mean, he wasn't that dark but he wasn't nowhere near light either. This nigga was my complexion.

My eyes was low and red. I was cheesy as hell. The gas I was smoking had me feeling good as fuck. Today was my ma'dukes 39th birthday, and we had got her the car she wanted and now we were treating her out to eat. We ain't really have that much family and didn't really fuck with nobody so it was just us three. My little sister Amari was meeting us here in a few.

"Boy hush and come on." My dukes said slapping Tana in the back of the head. She was five feet three inches and skinny as hell. Meanwhile, me and my twin was six feet and six inches. We were both cocky. Tana was bigger than me; he was about two hundred and fifty pounds. All muscles though. He was the big nigga. Santana had a scar on his face from when we were younger and he fell thru the glass table. He kept his hair on a short fade with waves, meanwhile I had dreads. I kept them braided or in a bun. Santana got tattoos all over his body and I had none. I also had a mouth full of diamonds. He just had a bottom gold grill. Only thing that could tell us apart was the tattoos, the mouthpiece and the hair. We were both two totally different people.

Santana was anti-social as hell and a show-off. I was cool with whoever didn't cross me and laid back. We was only nineteen, but we ran the streets like old niggas. The youngest in charge and was building our empire up to be the biggest, richest and rawest drug empire it was. We weren't there yet but we had a lot of status. Especially since we made the move to get some powerful people under our belts. Santana took care of the guns while I took care of the drugs. That's how we ran shit.

· · ·

It's always been me, my brother, Madukes and sister. Amari was only a year under us and the smartest too. She was part of our empire but we had bigger plans for little sis. Amari was in her first year in college and lived on campus. Right after college she was jumping to law school. That's what she wanted to be and we were supporting her hun grand. Our pops got booked when we was just five, and then a year after that he was killed. My momma took it hard but my siblings and I didn't really care. We ain't know or remember him. We for sure wasn't gonna miss nobody we didn't know. It's always been Madukes and us and that was our heart.

"What you over there smiling about?" My momma asked me as we got seated.

"Nothing, just thinking. You like yo car?" I asked smiling and she did also.

"Yes, I love it. Thank you guys so much. I love y'all." Mary said and wiped her fake tears. She was extra as hell but that's just her.

"How y'all been though? I just been seeing y'all less and less now that's it hot." She said and looked at Tana. He wasn't paying attention though; he kept looking at a table behind us and then he'd look away.

"Ma, you know we tryna get it. We gone be by more though, promise." Santana told her and I agreed.

"That's all I want." She told us and Amari came rushing in.

"Sorry guys. The traffic was horrible ... Hey mommy. Happy birthday again." Amari said all in one breath handing my mom two bags from the Louis Vuitton and another gift bag with balloons tied to it.

"Thank you baby. You didn't have to." Our mom said and grabbed the bag.

She opened up the gift bag, and it was a necklace we all decided to get with matching earrings. The other gift bag was a scrub outfit since she was a registered nurse. She decided not to open the Louis Vuitton boxes yet.

The waitress came over and we all decided what we wanted to drink and order to eat.

Ring, Ring, Ring.

I sighed and glanced at my phone. It was a private number so I ignored it but it did nothing but call right back. I excused myself and answered it when I got by the bathroom.

"Who dis?" I answered.

"This is Shante. Can I speak to Montana?" The girl asked and I sighed.

"This him. What's up? What you want? Who this is again?" I wondered and she sighed.

"This Shante. Look, I don't know if you remember me but I met you about a year ago and some...In Atlanta. Look, I'm not sure because to be honest I was drunk as hell. We both were. I had a baby a few days ago ... Twins... I'm just asking can you come and do a DNA test. I only slept with my boyfriend and you. He tested my babies and they weren't his. I have been searching high and low for yo number and just now finding it. I can send you pictures of my kids, I don't care if you don't want to be in they lives or whatever. I just needed to know and let you know." Shante voiced and I laughed.

"Man, quit fucking playing ... Who is this for real?" I wondered and leaned up against the wall. "Quit playing or I'm hanging up." I voiced and she sighed.

"You know what never mind. I knew I shouldn't have called you. It's okay." She started to say and hung up. I looked at the phone and was in total shock. Was she for real? I glanced at the phone and went to my call log to call back but she had called private.

"Fuck." I hissed and went back to sit with my family. I couldn't even enjoy myself. My thoughts kept running to ol chick and thoughts of me having seeds out here in the world.

Later on that night....

"What's wrong daddy? You look stressed." This stripper chick asked.

She rubbed and massaged my shoulders as I sat on her couch. I been fucking with her for about two months and this my first time coming over to her crib. I ain't really know shorty like that so I made sure my strap was close. I caught too many niggas lacking with they pants down. I won't be one of them.

"I'm good... Wassup with you though?" I asked. She started to run her fingers through her hair nervously. *Strike One.*

"Come on baby. Let's take it into the room." Diamond said and grabbed my hand leading me into the room. On the way she grabbed the remote and clicked a button; slow music came on.

Strike Two.

Diamond pushed me in the bed and climbed on top of me. She started raising my shirt up and unzipping my pants at the same time. I hope this bitch ain't think I was getting naked. I was getting my nut and dipping. She knew the routine. I wasn't in a relationship, and I wasn't looking for one either. I had too much on my plate to be worried about a female. Diamond was a bad-ass chick no doubt. She was gun thick and light skinned with freckles. She worked at the club my brother and I went to do business at. She was a top strip-per. I don't even know if that's her real name to be honest. She was just a hot commodity at the club so I wanted to see what she was hitting on. Right now she was on her second strike. Third strike then she was out like a night.

She pulled my dick out and started to lick on the tip. I couldn't even get into it cause I heard a noise in the front room.

Strike Three.

When the bedroom door busted open I had already had my free hand wrapped around Diamond neck with my gun pointed to her head.

"Put the guns down or I'mma blow her head off." I spoke sternly.

The two niggas looked at each other then at Diamond. I just smirked because they knew they had screwed up big time. Before they could even look back to my way I had already blew both they brains out. Diamond screamed really loud, and I just snapped her neck. I sat on the bed and sent my cleaners my location. After fifteen minutes my nigga Juan was walking in with his crew.

"What's up boss. We got it from here." Juan said. I hurried and grabbed my shit then dipped. I had too much shit on my mind, and I was not bout fall victim over a bitch.

KNOCK, KNOCK, KNOCK, KNOCK, KNOCK

I glanced at my alarm clock and it read seven-thirty in the morning. I sighed and grabbed my pistol from my dresser. Santana was on the couch knocked out, and I wanted to punch that nigga in the head. He was knocked out and heard the fucking door.

KNOCK, KNOCK, KNOCK, KNOCK, KNOCK

"Who the fuck is it?" I yelled.

"It's IMPD." The men yelled and I stopped in my tracks. It's been weeks since I had to murk that bitch Ashley, well Diamond, whatever the fuck her name was. I know they weren't here for that. My team was A-One so I know they ain't leave my DNA in that bitch. I looked back to Santana and he was slipping on his pants. The nerve of this nigga.

"Did they just say IMPD? As in police nigga?" Tana asked and I nodded. I handed him my pistol and opened the door.

"Hello Mr. Young. I am Miss. Braylon Washington. I'm with Indiana Social Services." She spoke and I wasn't even paying attention to what she said. My eyes paid attention to those pink lips and them titties that sat up in her white shirt.

"Mr. Young, did you hear anything that I have said? DNA results show that you are in-fact the father of both seven month year old, Harmony and Rhythm. May we come in?" Braylon spoke. When I heard her say DNA and may she come in, I almost smacked her.

"I'm sorry but right now isn't a good time." I said looking at the police. She cleared her throat and said

"I'm not supposed to do this but how about I come inside by myself and my friends just wait out here for me." Braylon said and I nodded.

I opened the door, let her walk in and slammed the door in the police face. Little momma ass was on fat fat. She kind of favored the rapper Jessica Dime. Jessica was colder.

"I'm not sure what you have going on but I was told you didn't know about the kids. The children's mother was killed two weeks ago in a murder suicide. The mother, Shante Armstrong, was under investigation by social services. Apparently, the oldest of the twins, Harmony, was sexually assaulted by the boyfriend and authorities believe that's why he murdered her and then himself. Listen, all I have to do is view the home, you agree to a background and drug test, and we can grant you full custody. If you deny any of the three, the children will go to next of kin. Sadly to say, in this case, it's no one. So they will go to a foster home until we can find a home that wants to adopt two babies." She said all in one breath.

"Aye listen, I know this is totally off subject but you was with shorty a few weeks ago at Olive Garden wasn't you?" Santana asked and sat down next to the chick.

"Excuse me?" she asked and looked at him then me. "Y'all twins? Wowww." she lowly said and Santana smiled.

"Yeah, I have been trying to get with shorty but she ain't been trying to give me no play." He said and I shook my head.

"Excuse my brother ma. I will do anything to get my seeds. You feel me? Shorty called me and told me but I ain't even believe her. I want my kids. When can I meet them?" I asked straight up.

"We can schedule you a drug screening today at five if that's a free time for you and I can come back. Let me see...." She clicked through her phone and smiled.

"I can come back same time tomorrow matter of fact and get an inspection. I would say by the end of the week we could have Harmony and Rhythm in your care." She said smiling.

"Thanks shorty. I would love that." I told her signing for the background check.

"Okay, Mr. Young, I will see you tomorrow then and don't forget to take this paper when you do your drug test." Braylon handed me a paper and stood up. She scribbled something on a sticky note and handed it to Santana.

"Her name is Aja and don't tell her I gave you her number." Braylon said and left. Little momma was sexy as hell. After she helped me get my seeds in my care I was gone make her they step momma. On the other hand, I was utterly shocked. Damn man. What the fuck was I gone do with two kids man?

AJA

. . .

"Awww fat man." I cooed as I watched my son crawl to me. He was smiling and drooling all over himself as he showed off his skills.

"That boy is on go." Granny Laura boasted as she sat in her rocking chair smoking her cigarette. Laura was my father's mother. When my parents got locked up she took me in. She was my heart and really the only family I fucked with other then YaYa.

"Thanks grandma for watching him for me. I owe you big time." I said getting off the floor and sitting on the couch as I rocked Ashton. It's been a long seven months since the park incident. The hood was finally letting me get my ass beat die down. Every now and then bitches that done fucked Miles would throw slick shots about him putting his hands on me. It didn't matter because they couldn't whoop me and they knew that!

"I see you got that makeup on heavy." She said turning her face up and rolling her eyes.

"Not today Gran. I have a huge headache, and I'm not in the mood for it." I said.

"Girl, you know I'mma say whatever I want to say. So you can be quiet!" She said interrupting me.

"I don't understand how many times I gotta tell you to leave that damn no good, dead beat nigga alone! All he does is beat yo ass. What, he gotta kill you for you to be done?" My granny Laura asked putting her cigarette out.

"No." I lowly said and she laughed.

"Yeah, that's what he gone have to do. How many times he done broke something on you? Huh... Damnit!" She yelled standing up. "How many black eyes you done had? Shit, that bitch maybe permanently purple." My grandma snapped. "I'm sorry but I can't sit back and watch him beat you to death ...... Let yourself out." Laura yelled as she walked to the back.

I quickly wiped the tears away and ordered myself a Uber

home. The whole way home, I thought about the good times with Miles and wondered where everything went wrong.

Miles and I was high school sweethearts. We graduated together and was in love. When I got pregnant with Ashton shit between us slowly started to turn and Miles turned into a completely different person. At first I hid the black eyes and busted lips. I was so ashamed of the shit Miles did to me. Now it seem like everybody around me knew and judged me for staying with him. They didn't know Miles like I knew Miles though. They don't know the good in him like I do.

As of right now shit all his ass did was do me in. I didn't know what I did to make him treat me that way. I prayed daily that something changed in him because like my granny said Miles was gone kill me one day.

———

Walking into my apartment the smell of weed caught me by surprise. Since I lived in the hood I was on a section eight program. Everybody knows my office don't play around! If they even get a whiff of weed smell I was on the first thing smoking. Plus, I already had a few complaints and disturbance calls filed on me from the times Miles beat my ass! I sighed in frustration. I was so fed up.

"What the fuck is going on?" I asked Miles walking to the front room. He had a full house. I mean niggas smoking, drinking, and playing the game. Bitches chilling and dancing. Even a bitch came walking out my kitchen, with my fucking ice cream, eating straight out the container. I didn't say anything though. I politely took my sleeping son to my room and laid him in his crib. I set all my stuff down and went to my front room. Everybody was just mingling like I didn't just walk in.

I walked over to the entertainment system and turned the radio off.

"Everybody needs to leave. If my house still full when I get out the shower y'all going to jail!" I yelled and walked back to my room to take a much-needed shower. It was going on nine at night when I finally came home. I have been at work since six-thirty. I was tired, hungry and wanted to sleep. Thank God I was off for the next two days, and I was catching up on some much needed sleep. After showering for a good twenty minutes, I stepped out and was caught off guard by Miles sitting on the toilet.

"So where have you been all night?" He slurred drunkenly.

"Gone head on Miles. You know I had to catch the bus to my granny's cause you couldn't come get me from work." I sighed trying to walk past him and he pushed me backwards making me slip and fall from my body still being wet.

CRACK.

I heard my wrist crack as I hit the floor.

"Fuck." I cried out in agony. The tears welled in my eyes but I refused to let them fall. I wasn't giving this nigga no more satisfaction on hurting me.

"So I know this morning, when you left here you had on blue panties." He said throwing my clothes that I took off earlier at me.

"Miles, what are you talking about baby?" I asked seeing his face turn cold and his eyes turn dark.

"Bitch, stop playing with me. You had on blue panties this morning ... Why you come home with black panties on?" He yelled getting in my face.

"I....I don't know what you are talking about." I stuttered feeling the tears fall slowly.

"Okay, so you think I'm..." Miles didn't even finish talking. He just started punching me anywhere his fist would land. I couldn't even try to block his hands cause my wrist was broken due to me falling.

"Please Miles." I cried out but he didn't care; the punches kept coming. I guess he started to get tired because I felt a kick that knocked the wind out of my body. Followed by another kick that knocked the wind back into my body.

"Hellpp." I screamed but nobody came.

"Shut yo stupid ass the fuck up!" Miles snapped dragging me by my hair. He stood over me and I couldn't see out my left eye. I knew it was closed shut. He kicked me in the face and my head hit the sink. I tasted blood in my mouth before everything went black.

"Ma Ma." I felt slobber fall on my cheek, followed by baby taps. My head felt like it was on fire and my whole body was heavy. My body felt like it was ran over by a truck and I was still lying on the bathroom floor.

I reached for Ashton and a wave of pain shooting through me as my hand went limp..

Crack.

Yup, my wrist was completely broken. I cried out in pain as I pulled myself up with my other hand and Ashton crawled to me. His diaper was super wet and booboo was running down his legs and back. That told me that I must've been knocked out for a while and Miles left Ashton with me. Groaning from the pain, I grabbed a wash towel with my good hand and wiped Ashton as good as I could. He started to cry, so I pulled myself to stand up. I couldn't help but cry out in pain.

I was even scared to look at myself in the mirror. My body felt so bad I know I had bruises all over me.

After making Ashton a bottle, I gave it to him which he gratefully accepted and started to suck the life out of it. That made me cry even worse. My son was hungry, and it only took him five seconds to devour that bottle. I made him another one and he drank that one, too, without throwing up. I slipped my son's clothes, a coat and a hat and gloves on. I was moving real slow but I prayed to God the whole time. Praying that he got me out this situation before Miles came back. It was mid-December so it was cold out. I didn't even have the strength to make him a bag so I just slipped on some pants and threw on a jacket. My body wouldn't let me put on a shirt or even under clothes. I had to get out of here before Miles came back.

I cried and cried every single time my wrist moved a certain way. I just wanted to chop it off myself so it wouldn't give me more pain. After slipping on some boots, I put Ashton's milk, a few diapers, and some bottles into my purse, grabbed my son and limped out of the house. I banged on the neighbor's doors, but I knew they wouldn't answer. It was the hood; everybody minded they own business except when it was them. Soon as the cold air hit me, Ashton started crying which made me cry. I couldn't find my phone so I'm pretty sure Miles took it. I just needed to get to a phone so I could call my grandma or anybody. I knocked on a few neighbors' doors, but I knew they wouldn't answer. People in the hood minded they own business to a certain extinct.

I walked for about two blocks passing store after store that was closed down due to it being six in the morning. I cried and screamed for cars to stop and help. If I wouldn't have thought somebody in the hood would shoot first and then ask questions I would've knocked on somebody's door. When I reached the neighborhood center, I knocked until I couldn't no more. I curled up against the door when I saw a light on in the office. Ashton started to cry and wiggle out my coat, but I held him close and zipped him up in it so he could have body heat and warmth from my coat. I banged on the door and when nobody came I sat down on the ground right there. My body slowly started to shut down and the last thing I heard was my son's cries as I passed out.

Chapter Four

SANTANA

Walking into the warehouse, I smiled big as I saw packages getting weighed and moved out. The west side of the building was going down to the west coast. Then the weight on the south side of the building was getting shipped out to the south coast and so on. My niggas had the warehouse jumping. I smiled and rubbed my hands together like I was bird-man. My shit was going smooth like always. My two main workers, Lucky and Tez, walked in with two duffle bags a piece. I sighed and shook my head. I already knew what it was.

"What's up?" I asked crossing my hands in front of me.

"We have to shut down shop. Some work came up missing and niggas coming up short." Lucky said and I nodded.

"I ain't ask no questions. All them niggas done for." Tez said and they handed me the bags. I opened it and the drugs and money was in each.

"Right on bulls. Take over B street." I told them and handed them a stack. They accepted the cash and went on they way. I dialed Montana and waited for the phone to connect.

"Some shit happened and shop was closed down out north." I told him and he nodded.

"I already know. You got dat?" He asked talking about the money and shìt.

"Yup, slide on me." I told him and we disconnected the call.

Ring, Ring, Ring.

"Hello?" I answered.

"How you doing Santana; this is James. I'm calling about the case you have me on with Clevon Johnson?" The lawyer I had working on my youngin CJ case said.

CJ was my guy when he was running for me, and I saw a lot of potential in the youngster. I just hate how he got caught up in his mom shit.

"Yeah, so how it's looking?" I asked standing over the balcony.

"It's going good for the most part. I'm trying to get the murder to self-defense. You know how these White people are trying to send another Black man to jail. I got him though. I got his case to get back in front of a jury. So when they set a date I'll let you know." He told me and I thanked him then disconnected the call.

After handling some much-needed business at the warehouse, I went around to the spots to see how they were running. Everything went smoothly so I stopped in on my little sister. She was in school still so I went to her campus.

Stepping foot on the college grounds it wasn't too live. Soon as people saw me pulling up in my brand-new Range Rover everybody wanted to see who it was. It was just my luck my hot inna ass little sister was walking out her building cozy with some nigga. I stayed in the car though watching them interact.

Everything went cool. So I got out the car as she was getting into her car.

"Who you?" I asked scaring both them.

"San? Uh what you doing here?" She asking backing up.

"Nah little sis. Who the fuck is this nigga? Matter of fact, why was you hugging on my little sis?" I asked straight up.

"This is my boyfriend San. His name is..."

"I don't give a fuck what his name is! I asked why was y'all hugging?" I asked and she sighed.

"Santana, this is my boyfriend Avery." She said and I smirked.

"Nice to meet you kinfolk." I told him and held my hand out for him to shake.

After we got the formalities together, I went up to Amari apartment and we chilled for a few hours.

Promising to take little sis shopping this weekend I went straight to the crib.

Chapter Five

AMARI

When my brother left it felt like I let go of the breath I didn't know I was holding. I couldn't believe he found out I had a boyfriend.

Avery and I have been dating for about seven months. He moved to my school last year and ever since we have been kicking it. Avery was really my first boyfriend. Even though I knew nothing about being a girlfriend, Avery and I was going... well Avery wasn't shìt! I know he ain't shit but he was my boo. I was used to him.

"Babe, what? Were you nervous?" Avery asked and I laughed.

"Yes! You don't know my brothers like I do. San was cool but Montana. Yeah, we not gone tell him yet." I told him and he smirked.

"Yeah, we are gonna tell him. You make it worse having secrets." Avery said and I nodded.

"Okay then." I smirked and my phone started to ring. I glanced at the clock and it was eight o'clock. I sighed and grabbed my phone.

"Hello." I answered.

"Hey girl. What are you doing?" Deja asked.

"Nothing, chilling with Avery. What are you doing?" I asked and grabbed my towel so I could shower.

"Girl nothing. I think I'm pregnant." Deja said and I rolled my eyes. Deja and I have been friends since we were in elementary school. Since she lost her virginity in the eighth grade, her ass been pregnant about six times. Nobody had time for that.

"Bitch by who?" I laughed.

"Okay bitch, don't start. It's a secret. He said he didn't want anybody to know until we come out." She said and I smacked my lips.

"Well, come over in the morning so we can go to the clinic." I told her.

"Alright bet. See you in the morning sis." She said and we disconnected the call.

Stepping into the shower I washed my body for about twenty minutes. I wrapped my towel around my body and slipped my slides on.

Walking into my room Avery was gone and I looked around my apartment for him. I sighed and went back to my bedroom. Avery always just got up and left at any time or any day. So I was used to it. He had a sick mother, so that was his excuse most of the time. I wasn't dumb by far. I just didn't care.

I slipped on some boy shorts and a tank top. I grabbed my keys, wallet and phone and walked out the door. On my way across campus I dialed Avery number.

"Sorry babe, I had to leave. My mother fell down the steps and you were taking too long in the shower." He said once he answered the phone. I rolled my eyes and walked to his dorm. I watched as Avery let the door open for his ex-girlfriend Sam while he talked to me on the phone.

"Okay bae, my mom is calling my name. I have to go." He

said and I hung up. I shook my head and walked to the opposite side of campus.

KNOCK, KNOCK, KNOCK, KNOCK!

"Who is it?" Charlie asked.

"Me." I yelled and the door flung open.

Charlie was so fine, standing at about 5'7, with a mouth full of gold teeth. He had tattoos all over and had the prettiest face.

"Wassup shorty?" Charlie smirked and I shook my head laughing. Charlie grabbed me by the arm and closed the door, pinning me to the door.

"Why you keep playing with me? Running round with that bitch boy." he asked. I could tell just by looking into his eyes that it was hurtful to see me with Avery. Not gonna lie, Avery was who I was with but Charlie has my heart.

See Charlie and I have been best friends since we were babies. Charlie's dad and my dad was real close. Both our dads died and that made us grow closer. Everybody just thought we were friends.

"That's you. You wanted me to be a secret." I said and smacked my lips.

"You been fucking him?" Charlie asked.

"You been fucking Kyra?" I asked.

Silence filled the air and I sighed.

"I don't even know why I came over here." I sighed and turned to walk away. I paused for a second thinking Charlie was gone call out to me but *she* didn't. She let me walk away.

Chapter Six

BRAYLON

"Look, you don't understand. This isn't like her! That nigga did something to her!" I yelled. The officer just looked at me then Skylar.

"Listen, we can't just go off he say she say. If it's probable cause we could issue a search warrant but your friend only been missing for what?" He asked and I sighed.

"Nigga, she been missing for a month now! We have not talked to her! We don't know where she is. I work with her. She hasn't even been to work!" Skylar shouted and the police man shook his head and pulled out his notepads

"Give me her information." He told us.

"Aja. A – J – A Harris. Born, November 11,1998. Here is a picture of her and her son. He's missing also." I started and he took the photo.

"Let me get your information and I will look into it." The police replied nonchalantly.

I rattled off all my information and he took it down. I sighed and Skylar followed me out the police station.

"What we do now?" Sky asked me, and I shook my head and shrugged. We hopped into my car and headed to the projects to see if Laura, Aja's grandma, had heard any news. Aja was missing and had been for a few weeks now. This nigga Miles was running around with any and every bitch that wanted his funky, lame ass. He even had bitches in my girl crib! That's not even the worst part; this nigga wasn't even worried about my girl being gone. I put all my money on this nigga knowing exactly where she was. I was afraid of that answer though! If my girl was dead, I'mma kill that nigga with my bare hands, and I put that on my momma.

Pulling up to Laura's house, YaYa, Aja's cousin, was pulling up too. We all hugged and walked to the porch.

"I'm guessing y'all haven't spoke to Aja either?" YaYa asked and we shook our head.

"Nope. We just went to the police station. They don't even give a fuck." Skylar said and I cringed.

I prayed for my best friend and nephew was okay. I wouldn't know what to do if they were dead somewhere. Laura pushed the door open, and I could tell she was stressed out like us.

"God. I knew he was gone do something to that girl!" Laura said and I sighed.

"We not gone give up. They are not dead." I added.

I didn't even believe my own comment. I didn't know if Aja was dead or not. I just prayed she was alive and just ducked off somewhere.

After chatting with Granny Laura and YaYa, I told them I was getting ready to hit the block and see what's up, so Skylar and I left. My phone started to ring and I sighed. This nigga was mad annoying and every since I met him a few months ago he been heavy on my line! I knew homie was heavy in the streets so I needed to holler at him and see if he could find some information out on my girl.

"Hello?" I answered.

"Wassup shorty. I been hitting you up. Why you ain't been

fucking with me?" His sexy ass voiced boomed thru my car speaker and I smiled.

"I just been extremely stressed out lately. Wassup though?" I asked.

"Aw yeah. What's been stressing you out? I hope not no bum ass nigga." Mon voiced and I smirked. This nigga was already jealous.

"Nah. My friend has been missing for a few weeks. Shit, I feel like her broke ass baby daddy got something to do with it and the police acting like they don't give a fuck." I told him and he was quiet.

"Then she out here somewhere with her baby man. It's stressing me out. I hope my bitch okay." I said sadly.

"Shorty, give me a name and address. I'll get on it!" He told me and I smiled.

"Aja Harris. Her address two hundred and three North Lawson Ave. She stay in apartment D." I told him.

"I got you. Stop worrying. I'mma find yo home girl. I just wanted to call and thank you for helping me get my seeds. It's been a long seven months but I appreciate it." Montana told me and I smiled.

"You can properly thank me by taking me to dinner. I like everything." I told him and he laughed.

"Alright shorty. I'll pick you up at eight. Text me yo address." Montana said and we disconnected the call. I looked over at Skylar, and she was looking at me with her stank face.

"Bitch what?" I asked.

"You over there trying to get yo back beat in while I'm stressing about our friend going missing!" Sky played and I laughed.

"Bitch, do you know who that was? Bitch, he's going to find her for us. Whether they are dead or alive. He's gone get us answers!" I told her and she shrugged.

"Nah, who is he?" She asked rolling her eyes.

"You know Santana's the one that was trying to get with Aja the day of the block party? It's his twin brother Montana." I filled her in on how I met him. How he had kids he didn't know about, and I was a social worker for the case. Every since I got his kids in his custody, he had been trying to get me to go on dates and sending gifts to my job. I turned them down because I had to wait until the case was closed. As of last week, it was closed, and I was trying to get to know Mr. Young. I know once his brother found out that Aja was missing, he was gone fuck Miles' punk ass up! Besides, something in my mind telling me that, that nigga was the reason my girl was missing anyways! I hope somebody put a bullet in his head.

After riding around for a little bit longer, we headed to my house. I lived up north. It wasn't the best neighborhood ,but it wasn't like Sky's or Aja's either. I lived in a four bedroom, three bath house my grandparents left me when they died. Being the only grandchild, I was spoiled rotten. My grandma left me her whole insurance check which was about sixty thousand. My grandfather also left me an insurance check which was pretty much hundreds of thousands. After giving my parents each twenty thousand and getting the house renovated, I paid taxes and bought me a car. I put the rest of the money up and got a job. I could've not worked and chilled on the money for a few years. Instead, I started a bank account for my future children and every check I worked for went into that bank account. Of course I started Ashton a bank account. It's his stubborn ass mother who don't want to accept the money. I even deposited ten thousand dollars into Skylar's and Aja's account. Skylar greatly appreciated and immediately started to spend. Aja was stubborn as hell though. She said she would use it when she got away from that nigga and got on her own. That was just an excuse though. Only reason Aja would leave Miles along was in death sad to say.

Aja, Sky and myself have been best friends since the sixth grade. Our parents were all best friends and had kind of drifted apart after they graduated high school. We all kind of linked back together when we got to middle school. All our parents was locked up on the same charge. Conspiracies to murder.

My dad and Aja dad got first-degree murder, two counts. Yeah, it's a long story for another day.

Anyways, I'm the oldest out of the three. I'm twenty. I'm the youngest at my job at that. Everyone else is twenty-eight and up. I started working as a janitor for Children Services at eighteen, fresh outta high school. During high school I took college classes and got my master's degree at twenty and been working at the Bureau since. Now here I am.

"Have you talked to yo pops?" I asked hoping she said yes.

We never talked about the case our parents was facing because it was just too much and at a point in time, we were even into it over that. When our parents got knocked, I went with my grandparents. Aja went with hers, and Sky went into the system until Aja's grandparents could get custody of her. She thought we blamed her, which part of us did. It wasn't her fault her bitch ass daddy couldn't keep his mouth closed.

"Nope, and I don't plan on it!" Sky hissed.

She was more mad at her dad than we were. I mean, she should be mad but Aja family and my family should be even madder. He got us split up and our fathers sentenced to life. We might not ever see our O.Gs outside of prison.

"Have you talked to aunty?" I asked and she nodded.

"Every single day. I'll be happy when they get to come home." She told me and I nodded.

"A few more years. I can't wait either." I told her.

After wrapping my long ass weave, I hopped into a much-needed bubble bath. It was a little bit after six when I decided to get out. I sat at my vanity set looking at my reflection. My bright skin was glowing from the organic black soap I used. Skylar watched and coached me as I did my make-up. Once I got done with my makeup, I hygined myself down then slipped on some white lace panties. Yes, I believe white lace panties was only for virgins so that's all I wore. Yes, at twenty years old, I was pure and saving myself for marriage! That's just what my grandma instilled in me, and I agreed with her. I let some niggas top me off before but that's as far as it went. I slipped on a red fitted, knee-length body con dress with some black tie up the legs stilettos. I stood in the mirror and combed my hair down. I had a twenty-seven inch sewn in with a middle part.

"Wear these friend." Skylar said handing me some silver hoops. I slipped those on and slipped on a silver watch and necklace. Spraying some Juicy Couture perfume on I grabbed my purse and headed downstairs as my doorbell rang.

———

This nigga was a fucking fool man. He brought me to Denny's. Don't get me wrong, I loved the shit out they omelets but nigga... I was thinking something better. Shit, even Texas Road House was better than this. I was complaining right now but he was making me laugh and giving off good conversation. The waiter brought our food and my stomach started to growl. I ain't have time to complain right now. I'm about to smash. Picking up my fork, he stopped me from eating.

"Okay shorty, look this ain't even me. I hate this trash ass food. I just brought you here to see if you was gone fuck with me if I was a cheap nigga or not. Not once had you complained so that's a plus." Montana smirked and stood up.

He reached for my hand, and with the other he pulled out a fifty dollar bill and placed it on the table.

"We got reservations for somewhere else." Montana stated.

"Nigga, you a asshole." I laughed as we left out of Denny's.

When we pulled up to a place called Le Bernardin a seafood and cuisine place my stomach growled loud as hell. Montana drove a nice ass twenty nineteen Mustang. When we pulled up to the valet he gave the young, White man the keys.

"I know how y'all be. Don't scratch my shit. Don't touch my radio, and if any of my change or blunt roaches gone it's gone be a problem." He stated and the White man turned beat red. He hurried off and we entered the place.

"Two for Young." He stated and the lady nodded and we followed her to the back. I had Montana order for me because I knew nothing about this place.

"So tell me about yourself." He stated once we was seated and ordered our food. I wasn't even up to talking. I was just worried about how I was about to smash out.

"I'm the only child. My mother and father is locked up right now. My grandparents raised me, and they died about a year or two ago." I stayed sadly.

"I'm sorry to hear that. Tell me about your friend..." he asked and I sighed. I tried to keep my mind off Aja and Ashton, but damn if that nigga did anything to my sister, I wouldn't know what to do. Aja, Ash and Sky was all I had. I couldn't lose nobody else close to me.

We talked all night about any and everything until they closed the restaurant. We ate good, had a few drinks and it was nothing but good vibes the entire night. I was on cloud nine when I walked into the house. It was going on three o'clock in the morning, and I was tipsy and high as hell. I didn't even smoke. I was feeling good.

"Bitch, I thought yo ass was gone be missing next." Sky said jumping off the couch scaring the shit out of me.

"Damn weirdo, why you still up? Lurking in the dark and shit." I shouted. She started to laugh and laid back down on the couch.

"Bitch, I was asleep. Your drunk ass woke me up stumbling and dropping shit." Sky hissed clearly irritated. I sighed and walked the other way. I wasn't gonna let this bitch ruin my mood. I was going to sleep happy as hell.

Chapter Seven

AJA

"Girl, you better wake up. Your son is getting bigger." I heard a familiar voice say. "He's walking too." She added to give me encouragement. I heard a door open and shut.

"Look, there he go right there. Grown butt," The same voice said. The lady that kept talking to me I have been hearing over and over again. It felt like I was dreaming but I couldn't wake up. I felt the bed get low then baby taps.

"Ma ma. Ma ma." I heard my son baby talked.

I tried to reach for him but I couldn't find the strength. My body was so heavy it felt like something was laying on top of me and I couldn't move.

"Yes. Move them fingers girl." The lady yelled getting happy I believe.

"Wake up; your son needs you. I know your family is looking high and low for you! You are healing up nicely. Now it's just time for you to wake up." She whispered then kissed my forehead. The bed got light again, and I knew she was leaving me again.

"Wait, don't go. Wait!! Please." I cried out but she didn't hear me. I was left alone with silence and my thoughts. I

knew I was in the hospital or something. I was hearing moni-
tors but I couldn't even move my body. Was I dead? Oh God,
I was dead. I started to panic and move like crazy, and the
machines started beeping real loud. Then my eyes opened.
The only light around me was from the machines. Two ladies
busted through the doors and an older man was right behind
them.

"Calm down. Hey, hey, hey, calm down." The lady said.
That's the voice I heard. Her voice was so soothing, and when
she touched my arm I immediately started to cry. She hugged
me as the man started to take the tubes out my nose and
mouth.

"Hello, Miss Lady, I am Doctor James. I was called here
by Miss Mary. Do you remember anything?" He asked doing
my vitals. I knew we weren't at the hospital because the room
I was in was an actual room. Carpet, TV, regular bed and
regular covers.

"Mhm." I coughed clearing my throat. My voice cracked
and my throat was on fire. The doctor must've read my facial
expression because he walked away and then came back with
a cup of ice water and a bottle of water.

"What is your name?" The lady asked and I sighed.

"I'm Aja. Where is?" I cleared my throat and looked
around the room. "Where is my son? Can I please see him." I
asked, and Mary nodded to another girl and she left the
room.

"Everything seems to be fine. Your wrist healed fast and
nicely and bruises are gone. After you get a little physical
therapy and get your nerves going your body should be
feeling better. Give it a day or so." He smiled and walked out.

"I'm glad you up. I have been taking care of little man for
a few weeks, and I just want to say, I raised my kids. I ain't
trying raise no more. So get yo butt up!" Mary laughed and I
smiled.

"Where am I?" I wondered and she sat down next to me.

"You are at my house. You don't remember anything?" She asked, and I couldn't remember anything... I was getting out of the shower and then everything else was a blank.

"Well, I found you and your son sitting in the front of my center. I own the youth center on Twenty-Eighth Street. You were knocking and I heard the baby cry and I came to see what was going on and found y'all two. You were pretty badly beaten up." She said looking sad. I sighed and felt the tears stream down my face.

"Nope! You not gonna cry. You not gonna feel sorry for yourself and when my sister bring the baby in you will be happy and not show weakness." She stated, and I was shocked but I nodded. "You are a beautiful young lady. I don't know nothing at all about you but you are strong and I know you are a great mother! Don't feel discouraged yet. God got you boo." Mary said and hugged me.

It was a knock on my door and the lady walked in with Ashton in her hands. Laying eyes on my big boy, it was like the first time seeing him again. All the love came rushing back, and I know seeing Ashton was all the assurance I needed to get out. He was so big and smelled so good. His hair was braided to the back and my baby had hang time.

"Da da." I baby talked, and he started hugging me.

"He missed you as much as you missed him. I'mma give you a few more minutes then I want you to get in the shower. It's clothes right there, and it's a bathroom thru the closet." Mary told me and I nodded. She left out the room and I sat down on the bed while holding my son. All he wanted to do was put his head on my chest and lay, and all I wanted was to feel him close to me.

Every since I got my kids I had a different outlook on life. I wasn't glad that their mom was dead but I was glad a young nigga didn't have to deal with the common baby momma drama. I ain't even gon lie, dealing with two toddlers was exhausting as hell. I still haven't even told my momma about them yet. Tell the truth, I been having my kids with me for almost eight months and been avoiding my momma at all costs. They were not bad kids though. They were very mature to just be turning one a few months ago. Harmony was the oldest and very active, she stayed getting into everything. Rhythm was laid back as hell and just went with the flow. We was transitioning from diapers to panties, and Rhythm had it down pack. It was Harms that wanted to play and didn't wanna listen at all. They started walking about two months after I got them, and it was amazing to watch them grow. I thought it was kinda cool that I could dress them alike, because it reminds me of me and Santana when we were growing up. I loved this parenthood shit and wanted to thank shorty a million ways for getting me connected with my seeds.

Speaking of Bray, I been talking to shawty heavy, and I'm really feeling her. I'm forever grateful for her bringing me my kids and on top of that our date the other night was a plus. Her vibe and conversation is what kept me interested in her. I had my lil niggas looking for her friend Aja cause it was really stressing her out so that's the least I could do. Speaking of her friend, my lil dude was calling me right now.

"What up lil nigga?" I answered.

"Aye, I found chick. She was closer than you thought big homie."

"Word? Where was she at? Is she alive?"

"Yeah, she alive. She doesn't even look like she was missing." He voiced.

"Aw Yeah? Send me a location so I can get the info to my brother. Come by the spot tonight. I got you!" I told him and we disconnected the call. I dialed Santana right away.

"Wassup brother?" He answered on the first ring.

"I found that chick you was tryna holla at. Why don't you roll down on her and see how she is before I let my shawty know that she's found."

"Say no more. Shoot the addy." He said and hung up, ol arrogant ass nigga.

I hit Ronnie phone and asked him where she was because he never told me and he said the neighborhood youth center. I laughed and relayed the message to bro. That explained why shorty didn't look like what she has been through; she was under the wing of our mama.

Santana arrogant ass was gone get a kick out of this. He texted me back and said, "That's right up my alley."

This nigga! I was also taking the girls to meet my momma on Sunday. She invited us over and hopefully I could get Braylon to go with me. I whipped the girls up some eggs and turkey bacon with their favorite, apple juice. These kids had me doing shit I never did before like waking up early as hell cooking breakfast, shit cooking period! I made two plates and set them at their Paw Patrol table and went to awake them. When I made it up the stairs, they were already both woke and standing up in their cribs. When they saw me they both had their arms out for me saying "da da".

I sat them both on the bathroom counter and washed theirs faces, brushed their teeth with no toothpaste on the brush. It's the thought that counts I guess. We proceeded down the steps and Melody sat in the chair with the girl dog Sky, from Paw Patrol, while Rhythm sat in the one with Everest. They begin eating using their forks more so than their fingers and I just looked on in astonishment. I swear I watched these little girls learn more and more each day.

"If only I had my shorty on the side of me to enjoy this moment and my life would be complete. I don't know what it was but she had me intrigued to learn more about her. She was gone be mine; she don't have a choice." I thought as I dialed her number.

SANTANA

When my brother sent me the information on little momma I sat on it for a few days. I didn't know what was going on with shorty, but I wanted to know what made her go MIA for these past few months. She had me intrigued, and all I have been thinking about was her thick ass. I wasn't even supposed to be checking for Aja with the way she dissed me the first time we met. I had to see what was up though. That's why I'm here to give her another chance. Yeah, it sounds cocky but I couldn't help it. Plus, I know it was more to her than just that buster. I need to see what she is about.

I decided to dress casual so shorty could feel comfortable

with me rolling down on her. I threw on a grey Nike fit with a red T-shirt underneath and my grey, white and red Air Max 95s. My mama hasn't told us nothing about her having someone in her house, and I was so curious to find out the story behind how they got to this point. I hopped in my all-black Charger with the red rally stripes and scurried off to my moms' crib. I got there in about fifteen minutes and when I pulled up it was a lil boy about one years old playing in the front yard with a ball. As I got out the car Amari came walking out the front door.

"Wassup sis?" I greeted her first.

"Nothing big head. Just visiting mama. What are you doing? She told me she ain't saw y'all since her birthday nigga!" Amari said putting her hands on her hips.

"You of all people know we been real busy. It ain't like we don't call and check in." I replied rubbing my waves.

"Whatever. Don't forget why we hopped in the streets in the first place! Don't leave my momma out!" Amari snapped and went to go play with the little baby.

I smacked my lips and walked in the house. There she was sitting there on the couch looking beautiful as ever. She lost a couple pounds but gained them back in all the right places. Her stomach was smaller and she had a lil more ass than before. I didn't know how to approach her so I just walked away without her noticing I was there. I found my momma in the kitchen cooking.

"Who are you and why are you in my house?" My mother joked smiling.

"Whatever Ma. What's up?" I asked and she kissed my cheek.

"Nothing much. We just walked in the house. How have you been?" My mother asked, and I smiled sitting down next to her.

"I been cool ma. Sorry I haven't been around. Trying to

get to this money." I boasted and Aja walked into the kitchen with Little Man right in front of her.

"Ma" He baby talked and raised for my ma dukes to pick him up.

"Uh... I'm sorry to interrupt. Mari said she's going to the grocery store. She'll be back in an hour. " Aja said looking at me. Our eyes connected, and I know my heart skipped a beat.

"Y'all know each other?" My mama Mary asked.

"No."

"Yes." We both said at the same time.

"Can I speak to you in the back for a second?"

"Me?"

"Nah, that owl." I said to her.

"Sure. Do you mind watching him?" Aja asked my mother and she shooed us away smiling and giggling. Aja switched off, and I couldn't help but look at her hips sway from side to side. I followed her to my moms' guess room which from the looks of it is where she has been staying.

"Ma, I been looking for you. Yo friends and family been worried about you. What's been up?" I asked her straight up. Aja started to mess with her fingers and that told me she was nervous. "Just tell me, how'd you end up here?" She sighed like it was weighing heavy on her and now I was really intrigued.

"Are you coming to put us out?" She asked. It caught me off guard because of the hurt in her voice.

"Nah shawty, I'm here to find out what's going on. We been looking for you."

She was shocked to hear that we was looking for her. Shit, I really was curious on how the hell a female that dissed me ended up in my mama crib. I know it had something to do with that weak ass nigga but I wanna here it from her mouth.

"You was looking for me?" She asked but I didn't say anything. "I had come home after working since six in the

morning. I was tired as hell. I was expecting to come home
and go to bed but I got the complete opposite. When I
walked in, I was met with the smell of weed, niggas drinking,
and bitches dancing." she paused and started to cry. Her eyes
were closed and lips was trembling. She was reliving everything that happened just to tell me. I didn't know if I wanted
to comfort her or not. I decided to wait and listen to the rest
of the story before I made a move. Once she pulled herself
together, she continued.

"I told them to all get out and they had til I was done in
the shower. When I stepped out the shower ... He... He was
sitting there drunk as fuck. He accused me of having a
different type of panties or something. Before I knew it he
was beating my ass. Punching me all over my body, then it
turned into kicking. I didn't try to defend myself because I
had slipped out the shower and bent my wrist back; it was
hurting so damn bad I knew it was broke. I hit my head and
next thing I knew I blanked out. I only woke up because my
son.... My son was tapping my head calling my name. His
diaper was so full it was busting out." She said turning her
face up.

"I got him clean and got the fuck out of there! I walked
and walked and I was in so much pain I sat down and ended
up falling asleep. Ms. Mary found us and saved us. I owe her
my life!" Her voice cracked. "I been at peace here. I didn't
know anybody was looking for me!" Her voice changed so I
could tell her getting it off her chest took a load off her.

"Damn ma, that's deep. I wasn't expecting that shit. I
mean, everybody knew he would be beating your ass, but I
didn't think it was nothing like that." I walked up on her and
pulled her in for a hug. Her moisture stained face instantly
soaked my shirt but her being in my arms felt so right at that
moment I knew I needed her. I told her I'd be back later on
that night. I was going to holler at Montana.

It felt so good to get that off my chest! I felt like a new person, and I was accepting my past. I felt something different when I hugged Santana verses when I hugged Miles. It was like an electric volt shot threw my whole body, and I loved that feeling. As soon as I told him what happened he let me know he'd be back later and to wait up for him.

I went to find Mama Mary and Ashton, and they both were knocked out on the couch. I took Ashton and laid him in his playpen we kept in the corner and put a throw blanket over Mary. Every since I been here I felt what it's like to be loved. I was just missing my homegirls. Ms. Mary is the mom I never had, and I'm so grateful for all that she's done for me and my son, because she didn't have to. She isn't looking for nothing in return. She did this out of the kindness of her heart. Even though I've been recovering well she still let me stay here, and she told me to leave when I was ready. I was going to go back to my job and see if they'll hire me back. Then I was gone get me a spot. Ashton was getting big, and quick, so sharing a space was not going to keep working. As the sun set, I started to straighten up.

Ms. Mary was in the kitchen starting dinner so I went ahead and gave Ashton a quick bath so that he could eat and get put down for the night. Mary cooked fried chicken, mac n cheese, green beans and corn mixed. We ate a home cooked meal damn near every night here in this house. Once we were done eating, I laid Ashton down so that I could shower. I stood in the shower about fifteen minutes before I lathered my body with Dove body wash that I loved so much. I didn't wanna be there too much longer because I didn't want to miss Santana's fine ass. I cut the water off and stepped out. After I pat myself dry, I coconut oiled my body down and slipped on my big T-shirt and boxers and headed back to my room.

Creeping into the bed next to Ashton my mind couldn't help but to drift off to Miles. He was dead to me but I thought about him every time I looked at my son, because they resembled each other so much! I wonder how fucked up the apartment was but then again I knew he didn't give a fuck about us or our place of residence. I hadn't seen no missing person alert on the news or anything which further let me know that he hasn't made any efforts to find us. As soon as I dozed off, I felt someone standing over me. I opened my eyes and damn near jumped out of my body. Santana stood over me, and I hated looking into his eyes because they were so unreadable.

"Hello to you, too." I said to him.

"Wassup. Aye you beautiful as fuck ma." He smirked licking his juicy lips.

"Thank you Santana." I said quickly turning away.

"Come with me real quick." he told me, and I got up and slipped my shoes on.

I knew Ashton would be okay in here sleep. Ms. Mary was always up creeping through the night. She'll eventually crack the door and peek in on him. The way her and Amari cracked jokes tonight on how much Santana likes me, I know she'll be okay with keeping an eye on my son.

I followed him out to the car and we both got in. Neither of us spoke any words the entire car ride. I had no idea where we were going but I trusted him for some reason.

We ended up deep in an area were I saw nothing but water. I gasped because of how pretty it was but also because I was scared. The moonlight reflected off the water so beautifully, and I had never seen anything like it before.

"You scared ma?"

"Yes, kind of. It's so beautiful though. It's mesmerizing." I spoke lowly.

"There's more where that came from." Tana responded.

I just turned to look at him. I could only wonder what he meant by that. We came to a gate that opened and drove some more before he turned into a paved driveway that rounded the house and led us to the back of the house. He opened the garage, pulled in, hopped out and entered the house. Well damn, just fuck me. After gathering my thoughts for a few seconds, I exited the car and went through the same door I watched him go through. The place was absolutely stunning, from the marble floors to the high ass ceilings. Everything was so nice and neat that you wouldn't have even thought this was his house so just to be sure I had to ask.

"This your house?"

"Nah, I broke in." his smart, arrogant ass responded.

"Come over here with me, ma. I need to holler at you." I proceeded to where he was and sat next to him on the sofa.

"About what?"

"You know one of yo girls be fucking with my brother. She's been worried sick thinking yo weak ass baby daddy got you up out of here." He revealed to me.

"Are you serious? I didn't think no one was thinking about

us." I told him truthfully. I was so excited to know my girls was taking steps to find me.

"You want me take you around there tomorrow to see them?"

"You'll do that for me?" I asked.

"Of course lil ma." Santana told me firing up the blunt he had been rolling since I sat down next to him.

"What do you want in return? I don't have nothing to offer. I'm poor and broke." I didn't want to be controlled by another man. I deserve better than to be controlled by any man. Ms. Mary told me I need to realize my worth, and I believe I'm starting to.

"I don't want anything from you. Like you said, find your worth and that'll make you a lot more attractive." He told me. I leaned over and kissed him before he could put the blunt back to his lips. I could tell I caught him off guard.

"I'm sorry. I been wanting to do that since you approached me that day at the park." I nervously laughed.

"You bold." He told me as he hit his blunt again.

I didn't say nothing else. I could feel myself getting hot from the embarrassment. It was silent until he finished his blunt off and then he continued on about what happened earlier.

"Come here." he said patting his lap. I climbed up on his lap and as soon as I was comfortable he grabbed my neck and pulled me into a kiss.

"I been wanting you since that day at the park but you dissed me for a lame. Now that he out the way, can you be mines?" I was speechless. I just nodded my head yes and kissed him again. Everything was moving fast but it felt right.

"Since you my bitch is it okay to fuck on the first night?" He smirked and so did I.

"I don't know about other bitches but with me? It's okay. Don't waste no time." I responded.

And that he didn't. In one quick movement, his dick was out and my panties were pulled to the side. He was sitting me down on it. He filled me so perfectly it had me in a bliss. He interrupted my thoughts with his moan. The shit was so sexy and that was reassurance that my shit was still popping. It was turning me on more than just listening to him moaning, and my moans were just as loud. I couldn't control my screams; it had been a long minute since I been sexed but never have I ever been done this way before. It was new to me, but I could get used to it though. The way Santana did my body, I knew he was feeling me just as much as I was feeling him. It seemed like he had a point to prove, because he sucked and fucked me so good.

Before it got too late, he returned me back to his mother's house. He didn't want me to leave him, but we both respected his mother too much for me to be coming in extra late. It was around three in the morning, and I knew I needed to get my two or three hours of sleep til it was time for Ashton to get up because once he was up, he was up. My phone dinged, and it was Santana of course.

Him: I need that in my life on the daily ma, I ain't gone front.

Me: you can have that and more. You make it home?

Him: word? And yea I'm here.

Me: definitely and okay ttyl. *I doubled texted.* That was amazing btw. I could get used to that.

I drifted off to sleep with him on my mind.

Chapter Ten

MONTANA

Pulling up to my dukes' center I stepped out feeling good. My hair was lined up and my baby girls' hair was freshly braided. They both were dressed alike In they little Nike outfits with they matching Nike's. I had to stop and take they picture as they slept. I grabbed Melody first because she slept harder than Rhythm. Then I grabbed the diaper bag and put it around my neck and grabbed Rhythm. Rhythm moved a little bit but laid her head on my shoulder. As we walked in, some kids was coming out.

"Hold the door youngin." I called out and the biggest one held the door.

"Hey Montana, them your little kids?" He asked and I smiled.

"Yeah. These my baby girls." I boasted smiling like a kid in the candy store. Melody raised up as she heard the noise and started to wiggle. They were always on the go and was ready to get into something.

"Come on Mel." I called out as we walked towards the back where my dukes was most likely at.

. . .

KNOCK, KNOCK, KNOCK, KNOCK, KNOCK!

As we were walking into my duke's office, Rhythm's head popped up so I let her get down and walk also. They were some independent little ones so they walked in front of me. Being nosy.

"Hey Montana. I was just heading out." My mama Mary said.

"I was just stopping by."

"Okay. Who babies?" She asked standing up looking over her desk. Melody went walking towards my dukes and my dukes paused and looked between us.

"I know. I know these not your.... Montana!! Who the hell you get pregnant?" She asked standing up. She kept looking in between Melody and Rhythm. Rhythm reached for my momma and she started to smile.

"They are gorgeous." My momma said and put them on her lap.

"Thank you ma. They have been with me for a few months now." I said adding on.

"Months?! Nigga what?" She asked and I sighed.

"They momma died and CPS came and brought them to me. I have been trying to make sure they are okay before I bring em around anybody. " I told my dukes and she shook her head.

"Oh goodness, I don't know what you and San gon do with two girls!" She laughed, and I shook my head.

"Ma, these little girls is something else. They amaze me." I said and sat down.

"They are so pretty Montana. They seem like some good babies." She told me and I nodded.

"They are. They are. You ready to be a grandma?" I laughed and she sighed.

"You having babies, Amari got a boyfriend. Santana all caked up. I'm getting old." She said smiling hard.

"Amari got a boyfriend? Don't get yo daughter hurt out here." I said seriously.

"Yes she does, and don't go messing with her either. You got two kids and neither of them is named Amari." My momma said but I shook my head.

"Yeah okay. Listen, wassup with Aja?" I wondered and she smiled.

"Aja has had a hard life. I keep telling Santana if he doesn't wanna do right by that girl then leave her be." She said rolling her eyes.

"He serious about shorty. Def." I told her and she nodded.

"Well, how is fatherhood?" She asked and I smirked. After chopping it up with my dukes, I slid down on little sis, so she could meet her nieces. Next, I was sliding down on Bray to see what was up with her since she had been avoiding a nigga.

BRAYLON

I had been avoiding Montana for the past few days. We had been moving too fast and I was slowly falling for him. He wanted to know why I kept pulling away from him but truth be told, I didn't know why. I just wasn't ready for a relationship right now.

Montana called me and told me he knew where Aja was and the only way he would tell me is if I went on another date with him. Don't get me wrong I was feeling him a lot but I needed to get my girl back before I jumped head first in this relationship because that's what I was bound to do. He told me I didn't have to dress nice and to look casual. I went with some high top jeans, a yellow crop top and the new multi colored rope Chanel sandals that had just dropped. I applied my lip gloss and was headed out the door.

It didn't take much for me to get cute, and sometimes, I did like the extra makeup and things but the natural look would do for today since he wanted me to be casual. I was so curious to find out about Aja's well-being. I was just hoping they weren't about to tell me they found her body, and that's why he said dress down.

When we arrived at this nice ass estate, I was immediately on alert, because why the fuck would we be coming all the way out to the middle of nowhere. I mean the estate was nice as hell. They had the nice round away driveway, bright green grass. Just a perfect house. As I was stepping out the car, Skylar pulled up. Now I was really confused. My heart was beating so fast and my stomach started to turn. I know these niggas didn't bring us all the way to the White people neighborhood to tell me my sister was dead.

"I brung you two girls here today because I got some news about y'all homegirl. Y'all ready?" We both nodded our head. It was a long pause, and now he was just stalling, and I couldn't handle the wait.

"Nigga, if she dead, tell us already so we can get on with the process." I told him.

"Follow me." We looked at each other and followed Montana. I know Sky was thinking the same exact thing as me.

"Get far the fuck away from here."

Walking into the house, my whole mood changed. The smell of soul food that I loved so much hit my nostrils. Soul music was playing in the background and laughter and talking was heard over the music. Montana grabbed my hand, and I followed him to the kitchen. Granny Laura was sitting at the Island with another lady, sipping wine.

"Hey granny." I weakly smiled and she embraced me, hugging Skylar right after. I looked around for Aja and Ashton but I didn't see a trace of them.

"Hey. I'm Braylon, and this is Skylar." I introduced myself.

"I heard so much about you girls. I'm Mary, Santana and Montana mother. It's finally nice to put faces with names." She said then hugged Skylar and myself. We both were shocked because Mary was gorgeous. If she wouldn't have said she was Santana and Montana's mom I wouldn't have known. Melody and Harmony came running through the kitchen, and I laughed when they both hugged my legs.

"Hey pretty ladies. " I cooed kissing they little hands.

"They here." Montana yelled coming into the kitchen. I sat down around the table, as the door opened and I heard laughter then stood up.

Tears came to my eyes when I laid eyes on my best friend. Aja had the biggest smile on her face, as she laughed at something Santana said. They looked like a happy family. Santana had Ashton on his neck and they all was rocking white. Aja's makeup was beautiful as hell, and she had a natural glow. She had on a nice, strapless, white flow gown, with some white sandals. Her hair was in its natural state, with a white headband. My best friend was gorgeous.

"Oh my God!" Aja shrieked when she saw us. First thing I did when I saw her was hug her then hug Ashton. It was an emotional reunion for all of us. I was just happy that my friend was back and healthy.

SKYLAR

· · ·

"Damn. You should've reached out to us!" I shouted as Aja told us what's been going on with her for the past seven months.

Yes, my bitch been gone for seven months, and we have been out here busting our ass while she was living good. I was mad but I was happier that she was alive!

"I wanted to badly. I was so fucked up though. The doctor even said he was surprised I even made it. It was bad y'all!" Aja responded.

My heart broke for my girl! She didn't deserve this type of shit. Aja's heart was golden and her soul was pure.

"Enough about that. I'm tired of reliving that situation and talking about it. It's out of my hands now." Aja said and sipped her drink.

"Yes hunny, anyways, you looking bomb." I said and smirked.

"I mean, this is that fuck nigga free glow!" We laughed at Aja's comment.

Santana, Montana and two other dudes walked in the backyard. I adored the way Santana looked at Aja. I mean, the way their bond was, it was like they had known each other forever. Aja told us they got real comfortable over the past few months, and I was happy about that. She needed something or someone to take her mind off that fuck nigga! She also said that he handled Ashton like he was his own. Plus, he was dicking her down good, and I can tell by the way she walked all up in here cheesing.

"Let me holla at you right quick shorty." Santana said picking Ashton up out Bray lap tickling him. They walked away like a happy family.

Montana sat next to Braylon whispering in her ear, making her laugh and blush. Leaving me lonely.

I didn't mind. I had other things to think about. My dad

been calling me for the past week. If you didn't know, my daddy was the reason why my life went crumbling down. My aunty Asia, Uncle Ray, and Aunty Trina was locked up for murder and kidnapping. Braylon's daddy Brandon was locked up also. It's a long story and, quite frankly, I hated talking about it. I knew I had to go see my dad soon though. He swear he has something important to tell me but I wasn't listening.

"Alright, so we all chilling out tonight? Y'all down." Aja said coming into view.

"Yeah." I said looking at my watch. It was a little bit after seven in the afternoon.

"I need to make a phone call." I told them standing up, dusting myself off.

"Damn." One of Montana friends said, as he checked me out. I assumed they were more of Montana friends cause they talked more to Montana then San.

"You strapped as hell little momma." He told me rubbing his hands together like BirdMan.

I rolled my eyes and smirked. I knew I was fine. I stood at five feet even. I was the smallest out the bunch but was the first to pop shit off. My skin was the perfect shade of dark chocolate and my facial features confirmed that I was indeed, mixed with something exotic. My nose was small but kind of pointy, my lips was full and big. My eyes is what stood out the most. They was big and doe-like but a bright hazel color. I always got teased when I was younger, cause I was real black with bright eyes. I knew I was pretty though. My hair was naturally straight, and it came to my shoulders. Yeah, I don't know what I was mixed with because my skin was dark as hell with some straight hair. My body was different. I had wide hips, a nice round ass that matched my hips but no stomach, and I had little skittles for breasts. Everything I ate went to my hips and ass, literally! I looked just like my mother, but instead she was a few feet taller than me. My height came from my father James.

"What's yo name Ma?" The same friend asked me but I ignored him.

He wasn't my type and even though I was dark as hell I liked them light. I hopped into the car with Aja and Braylon and we just chatted while we headed to Santana spot, I'm assuming. It was going to be a long night, I can already tell.

Sitting on the back of my truck, we laughed as Montana and Santana play fight. It was ten o'clock at night and we were having a good time.

"So what's been going on with you and Montana?" Aja asked Braylon and she blushed.

"What do you mean?" Bray smirked trying to play crazy.

"Girl boo! Quit playing crazy, we see it all in yo face!" I commented smirking and we all laughed. We all was tipsy and didn't plan to stop drinking until we were fucked up. All we wanted was to spend time with each other and have a good time.

That we did! We turned up all night long. I can tell at first Aja was kind of skeptical on drinking but after the third shot she was loosened up and I could tell Santana was liking it. We stayed up drinking and vibing until about three in the morning then we passed out anywhere. I mean, I was on the couch, one of Montana homeboys was on the floor. We was done for. I was happy though. I'm just glad my girl was back home, better than ever.

My alarm went off at five in the morning. I groaned and tossed the covers back. Stepping foot on my cold floor it creaked every few steps. It's been a few weeks since Aja came home and we linked up. I finally can handle what I been dreading to do.

Ring, Ring, Ring!

Just like clockwork the prison number flashed across my phone. I ignored the call like always and then an unknown number flashed.

"Hello?" I answered the first ring.

"Good morning." James' voice boomed through the other end.

"Good morning." I spat dryly.

"It's Saturday and just making sure you're up and on your way." He asked and I sighed. "Listen, you need to get here now and don't ask questions. You know my reach. Don't fuck with me sweetheart!" My father snapped and I cringed.

"On my way father." I yelled and hung up.

Walking through the heavy glass door, I followed the rest of the visitors. The guard led me to a table far away from everybody else and I sat down. My nerves was all over the place. I haven't seen or barely even talked to my father since I was twelve. What could he possibly have to tell me that was so important? My father was fucked up in the head. Growing up, my dad used to do so much screwed up shit to me and my momma it's sad even thinking about it. I couldn't even wrap my mind around why the hell my momma stayed with him for so long. It's been so many times child services was called to remove me from the home, but my mother talked her way out of it. I feel like that's why I get so mad when Miles fucks Aja up. I witnessed that type of abuse; I was a victim. That shit bothered me so much to know my friend was going through that.

My father walked into the room, and it seemed like everybody stopped talking. I was surprised to hear that my father snitched. If you knew James you knew he had a heart of a lion! Small but deadly and didn't take nothing from no one!

My father was very handsome; his complexion was a little lighter than mine, he had curly hair that he kept tapered even in lock-up. Tattoos lined his body, even some new ones on his face. My dad wasn't the normal father. He was a stone cold killer and you could tell by looking into his eyes.

"Hello Daughter." James smiled. I stood up and hugged him.

"Hey asshole!" I laughed and sat down across from him.

"You look beautiful baby girl." He complimented me shockingly. My father never gave compliments. Shit, I couldn't even remember the times when he told me he loved me. It is what it is though.

"Thanks dad. How have you been?" I asked and he sighed.

"Could be better. How has everything been going on the outside?" James wondered and I nodded. "Everything cool on my end, just working trying get a bag." I replied.

"That's good and how that's working for you?" He asked.

"What, making money?" He nodded and leaned forward.

"I got an easy job that can make you some easy, quick money." James said and I shook my head. His face turned cold. He started to tell me his plans he had for me. After hearing the numbers and that I would get paid upfront, I accepted a few jobs. I knew the money would come in handy. With how much we were talking, I can even quit my job! It all seemed so easy. I just knew I was gone regret this decision. Working with my Father was like selling my soul to Lucifer.

My father wasn't playing when he said he needed me to do something important. He texted me an address almost as soon as I left the prison. He said be here nine on the dot not 8:55 and not 9:01 but nine on the dot. I hit the corner that my GPS took me to. I slowed down until the time struck nine o'clock then hopped out the car. I had my gun in my purse off safety in case I needed to blast. I heard talking and followed the directions my pops gave me. I was surprised as hell though when I looked inside the apartment building and three niggas was sitting out chilling. I had on my black mini skirt that showed all my ass with a small ass belly shirt that didn't have any straps. On my feet I wore the highest heels I could find and my hair was pulled up into a bun with my natural face. I tucked my gun in my purse deeper and started stumbling and walking drunkenly. Soon as I opened the door, I stumbled purposely tripping over the first guy sitting on the crate.

"Man what the fuck shorty!" He snapped standing up catching me.

"So...sorry. I'm... I'm looking for door 5B." I stuttered.

"Damn little mama, you fucked up." The other dude said slapping my ass. I wanted to grab him by the throat and cut his hands off. I knew I had to play my role though. I giggled and turned around slowly, making my ass jiggle more.

"Hey. You cute." I slurred grabbing his hand, hugging him. He hurried and pulled my body towards him. Feeling up my skirt he raised it over my waist.

"Damn shorty." He whispered and I laughed.

"Help me find 5B." I playfully pulled away but he grabbed my arm.

"I got what you need shorty." The third guy said pulling out a wad of cash and my eyes got wide. "That sober you up. Come on." The same one said and grabbed my hand as we walked to the first apartment. I could hear the dudes getting hype. Shit, I can't even lie I wanted it as bad as they wanted it.

Soon as we entered the apartment, I was taking my clothes off. The first dude that I stumbled over, was pulling his semi hard dick our messaging it while sliding a condom over. He pulled me on top of him and he fell backwards on the couch. I laughed loudly playing drunk as he slid inside me slow.

"Shit!" I moaned out as the other dude was forcing his penis into my asshole.

"Fuck nigga." I cried as I felt his tongue slide in and out my ass getting it wet. After a few pokes he finally slid in and out loosening my asshole. I didn't miss a beat, though. I was throwing it back while getting my kitty beat in. I motioned for the last dude to come here. He walked up with his pants at his ankle stroking his manhood. I smacked his hands off and took him whole into my mouth, gagging and throwing it back. We went at it for about 15 minutes until I climaxed for the last time. These niggas had to be using they own drugs cause they was still going. The dude I was sucking off, pulled out my mouth then walked to the head of the couch and started to nut all over his friend's face. All thoughts went out the window when he yanked me off top of him in one quick motion and the nigga that was hitting me from the back started to suck my juices off his homeboy.

I looked on in astonishment at the scene in front of me. I quickly pulled out my pistol making sure my silencer was on and shot three times. Quickly killing them where they stood. I shook my head and laughed. For some reason seeing them niggas in action turned me on. So I pulled out my bullet and got myself off. Slowly getting my clothes on, I ransacked the house and found the stash. Whoever ran this spot was stupid as fuck. These niggas was sitting on major dough. I found four big ass trash bags filled with money. I grabbed two bags and then hauled ass to the car. I was scared as fuck and kept my strap close. If anybody came out, they were getting popped. I threw the last two bags in the back of the car and ran back to the apartment building. I grabbed the two half-drunk Hennessy bottles and threw it over the dead bodies. I had to be quick. I ran to the stove and lit the gas eyes and blew them out. Going into the front room, I lit a match and through it on the couch. I waited until the bodies was completely on fire before I got the fuck out of dodge. Soon as I got home I powered my phone and dialed my father's prepaid phone number.

"Hello?" James answered whispering.

"It's done!" I spat and he laughed.

"Good girl. You can keep the money." James hung up the phone in my ear. I looked in the back seat at the four bags of money and sitting right next to them was the floating faces of the three young dudes I just had to kill.

"Please forgive me Jesus."

Chapter Eleven

SANTANA

"You look beautiful shorty." I told Aja as I pulled her chair out. We was at this restaurant with the family. Little Man was with YaYa, Aja's cousin, and I had her all to myself. It's been about nine months since we been kicking it and shorty had me like putty in her hands. It took everything in her tonight to come out. She was so fucked up all she wanted was to chill in the house. She was even scared to let little man go anywhere. I tried to break her out of that and let her know she was safe with me. I was for sure gone handle that fuck nigga she was fucking with. He had her fucked up in the head and I was paying for it. I wasn't gone give up on Aja though. Shorty was special and I was gone make sure I showed her I wasn't like that other nigga.

Shit been going smoothly for us these past few months. She was opening up more and more and I loved that.

"Thank you babe." She smiled. We were all enjoying dinner and talking about the yearly back to school block party we were sponsoring.

"Yeah, we gone go this year. Just because I want everybody to know who's behind the scenes." Montana said and I nodded.

"Well my guys gone bring the stuff in the morning. Who's over it?" My mama asked.

"Dennis and Danielle. They got everything together." I told her and she nodded.

"Okay then. I'm proud of you guys." She said as the waiter came walking over the same time as Amari and her boyfriend walked in. I could tell Montana wasn't feeling it so I leaned back. It was about to be some shit right here. I smirked.

....

"Man, come on shorty. What, you're gonna be cooped up in the crib forever?" I asked Aja as I slipped on my boxers.

She was getting little man dressed and we were dressing alike today. I had put on some black True Religion Jeans, with a white, black and yellow matching True Religion shirt. Slipping my feet in my all white Ones, I made sure Aja slipped Ashton on the same exact thing with his little chain and bracelet.

"So that's a no?" I asked again and she sighed.

"Look ma, no pressure. I want you to be ready to get back out to the real world on yo own time." I told her and she forced a smile.

I knew that fuck nigga scorned her to the core. I wanted to get her out that shell she put herself in. Aja was beautiful on the inside and out. She also had big dreams for her future, and I wanted to be there for her, helping her reach every milestone. I ain't even gone lie though, Aja came in and turned my life upside down. For the better of course. She had me doing shit I ain't never ever did before. I'm talking about long talks, late nights on the beach, candlelight dinners, man rubbing her little chubby feet. Even the smallest things like running her bath water. Her thick ass had me wide open in so little time. I don't know how she did it. I was even being a family man. Treating her seed like he was mine came natural to me. All I wanted was to make shorty and our kid happy.

Ring, Ring, Ring!

"That's Montana. They must be outside." I walked over to Aja and picked Ashton up out her hand.

"Are you sure you don't want to go?" I wondered one last time before grabbing his bag and throwing it over my shoulder. "I can wait while you get dressed." I low-key begged. I wanted to be around baby girl all day if I could. That's how much I was feeling her.

"Okay, fine. Let me go slip something on." She hurried and stood up.

She kissed my lips as she went upstairs to my momma's guest room. Yeah, she was still at my madukes' house. I wanted her to move in with me, but she said she didn't want to rush anything. I was the one rushing,. Even had somebody baby proof the crib for when her and little man do come visit me. She had me wrapped around her little finger, and I'd give her the world or die trying if that's what she wanted from me.

Ten minutes passed and Aja came walking down the stairs. She was sexy as fuck. She wore a white sundress that had a slit on the side that came all the way up her thigh. Her hair was in its naturally curly state with a part on the side and some lime green Chanel oversized shades rested on the top of her head. On her feet was some lime green Chanel slides. Aja wore light jewelry and her multicolor Chanel purse on her shoulder.

"God damn shorty." I complimented and she blushed.

"Come on silly before Montana leave us." She laughed

fishing thru her purse. Before leaving out Aja grabbed Ashton bag from my shoulder swinging it around on hers.

Pulling up to the park, I glanced at Aja and saw that her body got tensed.

"You gon be alright shorty. I got you!" I reassured her, and Montana pulled on the side of us. Here we were again ,the yearly back to school block party. This time we had it at the park by my mom's center. We had the bounce houses and water slides for the kids, face painters and horses. A few grills going on and plus a back to school, giveaway. It was late July and it was hot as hell.

"Y'all did the thang. I love the theme." My momma beamed walking up on us as we stepped out our cars. That's crazy how things changed for us tremendously. We went from being head first into the streets to a year later being family men. We were still in the streets. Matter of fact, we were out here heavier than ever!

"Let me get y'all pictures right quick." My mama said.

I grabbed Aja by the waist and pulled her closer to me. She kissed my cheek while I had Ashton in my other hand. Meanwhile, Montana had Harms in his arm while Braylon held Rhythm badass. My brother thought his kids was sweet as hell but them little girls was baby Lucifer's.

"Come on shorty." I grabbed Aja's hand and pushed through the crowd with my momma following behind us and Montana and his family and friends behind him. People was recording and taking pictures. I could tell that made shorty uneasy so I squeezed her hand for reassurance. Everywhere we went in the hood this was how it was. My brother and I was well-known. The fact that we never really had women in our life was shocking to people. Then one day we popped out with whole families. Everybody was just as shocked as we were.

"You like hood royalty." Aja said once we sat down at the

table. Ashton was sleepy, so Aja pulled out the blanket and laid it under the tree and laid him on it. It was his nap time so I figured he would sleep for a good hour.

"Hey guys." Amari sang walking up with her group of friends. I groaned and kissed Aja cheek.

"I be right back shorty!" I grabbed Amari and her friend Deja by the arm and made them follow me. Dej was smirking and I wanted to smack fire from her ass.! "Bra why the hell you bring her? You knew Aja was gone be here." I hissed looking at Dej with pure disgust.

"I didn't know she was coming. Last time we talked she said she wasn't coming out." Amari said realizing some shit was bound to pop off.

"Go home Deja!" I yelled through a closed mouth.

"I'm not going nowhere! You not my daddy!" Dej shouted rubbing her big ass belly.

I mean, shorty was nine months about to pop. I fucked this ditzy ass girl one time and that was seven almost eight months ago, right before I got with Aja. Then the next week this bitch hit me with she pregnant. I be damn exactly one month after I cracked I saw shorty and she was already showing. I knew she wasn't fucking pregnant with my seed!

"Stay the fuck away from my shorty!" I snapped walking away.

A few weeks ago, Dej blew my phone up one night and I ignored it. Aja had saw and asked who was Deja. I wasn't the type to lie cause I truly didn't give a fuck what the next motherfucker thought about me but with Aja the lie rolled off my tongue fast as hell. I couldn't even take it back. I just prayed she didn't put two and two together. I sat down next to Aja and she handed me a cup.

"Ease up. You were worried about me but you look tense as hell." She giggled.

"Come over here to the grill with me Aja." Braylon said

pulling Aja away, and she looked at me like she wanted approval.

"What I tell you about that? Go head and do you Ma. I'm right here. I got little man." I told her as I sipped from the red cup. Aja stood up smiling and kissed my lips. I watched as she walked away.

"Damn boy, she got yo ass wide open." Montana joked passing me the blunt.

"Shut up nigga." I smirked and looked away.

Not for long, though, because I kept glancing back to where she walked off to. Every now and then she would look at me shyly and blush. It was like our eyes was magnetic cause we kept looking at each other. My mother walked over with my aunty Tasha in tow.

"Wassup aunty?" I greeted standing up hugging her.

"Hey guys." She replied back and sat at the other end of our table.

"I'm so proud of you guys." My mother said making me smile.

"I love the family look on y'all. You both have some beautiful women in y'all life with kids. Cherish that!" She told us and walked away. Ashton started to whine, so I stood up. He raised when he saw me.

"Da-Da," He baby talked and I laughed. I picked him up and looked back to where Aja was standing in line at. She wasn't there though so I scanned the crowd.

"Look at this nigga!" I heard Montana say, and I turned my attention to where he was looking at.

Aja was cornered in between her weak ass baby daddy and a table. She was searching the crowd for something and when her eyes met mine it felt like she was begging me to come save her. I held Ashton close to my chest as I made my way across the yard. The crowd parted ways as I could hear Montana telling me don't murk this goofy ass nigga in front of everybody.

"What's up wifey? You good?" I asked wrapping my arm around her shoulders. I mugged her weak ass baby daddy and dared he tried anything. Aja melted into my body, and I could tell this weak ass nigga really scared her ass for dear life.

"This you now?" He asked her apparently in his weak ass feelings.

"Don't ask my shorty shit! You got any questions for her you take that shit up with me my nigga." I snapped. His eyes met mine and for the first time he paid attention to his son in my arms.

"Don't look at my seed. Matter of fact, get ready to sign those rights over cause you ain't needed around these parts bitch boy." I taunted him.

"You got it big bro!" He nodded and took one last look at Aja then her son. He gave her the nastiest glare and walked off. Aja took Ashton out my arms and stormed off. I followed after her like a lost puppy and when we got to the parking lot, I finally grabbed her and turned her my way. Her tears were flowing and my heart broke as her chest felt up and down. She tried to wipe her tears, but I moved her hands from her face.

"Why would you say that? Why would you say that? He..." Her questions caught me off guard so I stood back then looked at her.

"What you mean Shorty? Say what?" I asked for clarification.

"You told him to sign his rights over. He's going to kill me. I know it. " She cried harder hugging her son closely.

"Man shorty, if you think I'mma let any nigga touch a hair on yo head you tripping! That nigga already got a bullet with his name on it for putting his hands on you in the first place!" I snapped and pulled her close to me.

"You not fucking with no lame baby. I told you from the

start I got you. I got you and him ma." I told Aja and lifted her head up so she could be looking into my eyes.

"I love you Santana." She whispered and I smiled like a kid at the candy store hearing those words.

"I love you too shorty." I smirked kissing her lips.

"Da-Da," Ashton reached for me and I took him from her arms.

"Santana ... I'm not going to feel a hundred percent safe until he is dead. I want him to die." Aja told me.

"Whatever you want from me, you got it wifey." I told her as we walked back to the family.

Pulling up to my dukes crib, Aja's eyes fluttered open. We stayed at the park having a good time until it got late. We ate food, chilled and just had a good ass time. Soon as we got in the car, Aja and Ashton was knocked out. "I thought we were going to your house tonight?" She asked yawning.

"I got to make a stop right quick. I didn't want to leave you home. I'll be back." I told her as I got Ashton out and got her situated in the house. I turned my phone off and threw it in the glove department as I made my way to my destination. Walking inside the building, I entered then went to the room I held my meetings in. Some niggas I never met before sat on the opposite side of me and Montana.

"What's up?" The nigga I know as Show greeted us, his brother Beans didn't say nothing and that was strike One. "What's up with you?" I asked Beans and he looked at me. I laughed and sat down next to Montana. "So what's up?" I asked them and Show stood up. "Shit, we came all the way from Michigan. We heard y'all had that grade A pure cocaine." He said and I looked at Montana. He nodded and I stood up and pulled my strap out. They both threw they hands up in surrender and I laughed. I searched Show then searched Beans making sure they weren't wearing no wires or had no phones or nothing else.

"Man." Beans laughed and I stood Back.

"What's funny? Enlighten me?" I smirked too.

I was ready to put a bullet in his head cause this nigga was too disrespectful.

"Ignore my brother. Look, we needed a Connect on the guns too. If y'all can help us we appreciate it ... if not we gone go on our way." Show said and I looked at Montana.

"We gone do business with you, not ya mans though." Montana said and I smirked.

"Come on, bro, we don't need these pretty ass niggas!" Beans smirked and I laughed.

"Go head on. Show if you wanna continue this business venture then holla at us." Montana said.

"Aye. Don't let that nigga stand in the way of you making yo bread homie." I told him, and Beans stood up and walked off.

"He a bitch." I laughed and sat down.

Brandon and Jamar walked in. They were my aunty Tasha nephews. Brandon and Jamar ran shit back in the day and definitely taught us everything we know.

"What's up cuz?" I asked shaking up with both them and they sat down around the table.

"Shit, chilling. We just got back in town. We wanted y'all to handle something for us." Jamar spoke and slid a duffle bag on the table.

"It's names, pictures, and addresses in that bag. It's one hundred and twenty bands in that bag. Sixty a piece. We want the whole family gone. When it's done, I'll wire a million dollars to both y'all accounts. Let's just say this a down payment." Brandon said and I looked at Montana.

"Y'all know this ain't even my style." Montana said and pushed his chair out." I laughed.

"This nigga. Alright, wire the two mil to me. I got you in three days." I promised and they smiled.

"My nigga! I told you." Jamar laughed.

"How the wives and kids?" I asked and Jamar smirked.

"They good. I heard y'all little niggas done settled down. We having a barbecue next weekend. Bring the ladies and kids." Brandon told us and we dabbed each other up. I grabbed the duffle bag and we all went our separate ways. Making a few phone calls, I got shit in motion for the next few days. I can already see shit finna get rocky.

MONTANA

"You being all secretive and shit. Just tell me what's up g. I'll leave you alone." I told Braylon as she gathered her stuff. This was an every week thing for shorty. Every time I think we moving forward here she go pulling away.

"It's not you... it's me. I'm sorry." She said as she grabbed her shoe and slipped it on. I followed her to the door trying to get her to stop and talk to me. I'm not gonna lie, her leaving like this did something to me. It was like every time she left she took my heart with her. Braylon don't even know how much I'm feeling her. I tried showing her love and affection but she act like a nigga. She showed no emotions, no feelings, and her communication skills sucked. I put up with it all because I was feeling shorty ass.

"Listen ma, if you leave out the door you might as well not even come back." I told her and she sighed.

"Montana, I have problems." She said lowly.

"I do too. That's why I'm here to help you." I told her straight up and she shut the door.

"You gotta trust me Ma. I'm all in." I told her, and she turned around with tears running down her face.

"It's scary. I love you Montana. I don't wanna keep pushing you away." Bray said and I smirked.

"I love you too." I pulled her close to me as we kissed.

Braylon came back to bed and we laid and talked about everything. She told me she had real bad trust issues and that she didn't trust many people. She was fucked up behind some shit that happened with her parents and I couldn't blame her. I always had my dukes and if something was to happen to her I would go crazy!

"I got you shorty." I whispered as she slept on my chest.

Ring ring ring ring!

Grabbing my phone off the nightstand, Santana's name flashed across the screen.

"Hello?"

"I'm about to pull up. Be ready." He said and hung up.

I kissed Bray forehead and snuck out of bed. Dressing in all black, I grabbed my favorite side piece and left. It was about to be a long night.

"Look, the drop I got is wild bro. You know them niggas Jamar and Brandon making dumb ass money. Bro, the niggas they gave me the hit on owe them niggas millions!" Santana said and I nodded.

"Jamar was making that bread back in the day." He added.

"He got his hands in the legal shit now." I told.

San then he nodded.

"That's how we need to get. We need to give this drug shit up." I told Santana and he agreed.

"I am. Give me like three more years. I'm trying to see where this shit headed with Aja." He told me.

"Speaking of Aja, how sis?" I wondered, thinking about the shit Braylon told me tonight.

"Man, she coo. She just shaken up. I need to get her baby daddy together. He be playing crazy." Santana said.

"Yeah, get him all the way together in this bitch." I said and we both laughed.

Pulling up on a dirt road, I could see an old factory up ahead. Santana cut the lights off and I grabbed the duffle bag in the back seat. We grabbed everything we needed and stepped out.

We both jogged to the building and just like it was planned it was a few cars parked. I shook my head and went to the back of the building. Santana cut the lights off and just as we headed to the front, niggas started coming out looking around. They didn't see it coming as we started emptying the clips hitting everybody that came out. All you heard was gunfire.

When the smoke cleared it was about 15 niggas on the ground.

We waited to see if more niggas was gone come out but nobody ever came.

Running towards the door, I peeped inside and it was empty. Santana grabbed my arm and we ran back to the car and got the fuck far away before the police came.

———

"You nervous? You look fine shorty." I complimented Braylon as she rubbed her hands down her pants.

"You not? My momma is cruel Montana." She said and I laughed.

"Girl, I'mma thug baby. I ain't worried about nothing." I told her as the doors opened and all the inmates started coming in. Braylon stood up as the last person came in. I could tell it was her mother because they looked exactly alike. I mean, down to the mole on the side of the lips alike.

"Ma." Braylon said as they hugged each other.

"Hey BrayBray." Her momma said and pulled away looking her up and down.

"You so grown and gorgeous." Trina said and smiled.

"Thank you. You look good too momma." Bray said smiling as she touched her momma's hair and face.

"Sit down. Sit down. Who are you?" She asked. I laughed and Braylon sat on the side of me.

"I'm Montana. I'm Braylon's boyfriend." I responded and she smacked her lips.

"Boyfriend. How old are you. Where are you from?" Trina asked and Bray sighed.

"I'm 20... I'm out west. 2g." I stated calmly and she nodded.

"What you want with my daughter?" She asked.

"She helped me get my daughters in my care. I just wanna love her and show her the world." I stated honestly looking at Braylon who blushed.

"I guess." Trina said and rolled her eyes.

"How have you been?" She asked and held Bray hands.

"You want anything ma?" Bray asked and Trina stood up. I handed the bag of change to Bray. They walked away to the vending machines, I guess to get privacy.

———

"I thought you going to see ya ma dukes was gone make you feel better." I told her and she sighed.

"I'm okay, Montana, for real." She tried to reason but I wasn't feeling it. Shorty been walking around looking a mess in her feelings since last week when we went to see her people.

"I'm really okay Montana for real." She said and tried to walk away. I grabbed her arm and she winced in pain.

"What's wrong?" I asked again and she tried to remove her wrist from my grab. I pushed her sleeves up and her wrist had slits on it.

"What the fuck Braylon!" I yelled pushing her away from me. "What the fuck are you on?" I asked and she slid on the floor crying in her hands.

"You really out here moving like that?" I asked, shocked that shorty wanted to kill herself. Or even did some fuck shit like cutting her wrist.

"I can't. I'm sorry, Montana." She cried through her hands and I shook my head.

"Shorty, come on now. You really trying to kill yoself?" I asked. She nodded her head yeah and I sat down in front of her.

"Why? Talk to me." I begged and she looked at me.

"I'm broken Montana. I don't know why, but I'm hurt right now." She cried and I pulled her against me.

"Shorty, you wanna talk to somebody? Talk to me? I mean, let me know what I gotta do to help you." I told her.

"When my parents first got locked down, I was diagnosed with Bi-polar disorder and major depression disorder. It's gotten better over the years but when Aja left I couldn't come out of it. I don't know what's wrong with me." She cried and I sighed.

"Are you taking your medicine?" I asked her and she shook her head no.

"It makes me feel sick. I'm not normal with it." She told me.

"Bray, you have to. If you doing shit like this then you gotta get back on yo medicine or you gone hurt yourself or somebody else." I told her and she sighed.

"I'm sorry, Montana. I just don't want to feel like this again." Braylon cried out and I hugged her.

"Come on, ma, we about to get you some medicine." I told her standing up.

I grabbed Braylon's hand as we went back to the room. I couldn't shake the fact that shorty was this fucked up that she wanted to kill herself to ease the pain. That shit was weak-minded and, to keep it real, it made me not even want to deal with Bray on that type of level. She needed to get her shit together for real.

SANTANA

"Bitch, quit fucking playing with me!" I snapped as we walked to the back room.

"Okay, so you just want a DNA test?" My aunty Janet asked.

"Yes. Don't tell my momma." I said and we laughed.

"Right this way." My Aunt Janet said and we walked into a private room, with computers and everything in them with a few men in white coats standing around talking.

"For real Santana? Are you for real? I said it's yours! I haven't been with nobody else!" Deja screamed. I shook my head and she handed the baby boy to my aunty Janet. Janet looked at the baby then looked at me. She stuck something in the baby's mouth and then handed it to a guy that put it in a machine. She did the same for me. Janet handed the baby back to Deja and she stormed off.

Every since a few months ago when Deja showed up to the park, I just kept my distance until she had the baby. She had the baby three days ago and, before she left, I made my aunty do an instant DNA. Yeah, money can buy anything, and I had to know was shorty baby mine. I knew deep down inside it wasn't because the times didn't add up. I just wanted it on black and white. Shorty storming out proved to me I was right though! That bitch wasn't gone pin a baby on me and think I was gone be a foo ass nigga and take care of it. I shook my head and reached into my pocket. After peeling off a few hundreds, I gave it to my aunty. She shook her head, laughed, and handed me a paper. Indeed the baby was 0.0000000 percent mine. I smirked and went on my way.

Pulling up to the juvenile center, I made sure all my jewelry and money was in my glove compartment.

RING RING RING!

Amari's name flashed across my screen and I groaned.

"Hello? I answered.

"Why did you do that Santana?" She asked and I laughed.

"Sis, stop hanging with thots! Shorty ass just tried to trap me with that baby! She knew it wasn't mine." I calmly said and Amari smacked her lips.

"Wow, Santana. See, that's exactly why I say don't have sex with my friends! I don't want to be in the middle of anything!" Amari replies and I laughed again.

"Sis... That bust down ain't yo friend. Shorty only wanted to be with you because she wanted to get close to me!" I told Amari straight up.

"Whatever. What are you doing?" She asked me.

"I'm on my way to ma dukes' crib. I'm bout to pick Aja up so we can go check on her friend." I told her.

"I'm pulling up there now." She said and we disconnected the call.

Chapter Twelve

AJA

"*You thought you were gone be able to get away from me. Better hope I don't find you and blow you and that nigga head off.*" I read the text message over and over again. I cringed just thinking about what Miles looked like texting that to me. I don't even know how this nigga had my number.

"*I got you bitch!*" He doubled text and I sighed.

I jumped up and made sure the windows were locked. I checked on Ashton and made sure he was sound asleep, and I went back to lay in the bed. It was only eight in the morning and Miles was on bullshit. I dialed Santana phone and he didn't answer, so I called my cousin YaYa.

"House of Beauty, this is Cutie with the big ol booty." She answered the first ring. I laughed and shook my head.

"Bitch, that's not how you answer the phone." I joked and she smacked her lips.

"I'm still mad at you, hoe. Don't call me like we coo!" YaYa hissed and she hung up.

YaYa is a hot mess. She was still in her feelings about me not calling her when that shit happened with Miles. No matter how many times I apologized she still wasn't fucking with me. I dialed her number and she finally answered.

"What Aja?" She asked.

"Girl, don't hang up on me. I wanted to tell you what's going on with Ashton." I lied and she gasped.

"What's going on with my baby cuz?" YaYa wondered.

"He's very sick. He wants his god mommy to stop being mad at his real mommy!" I joked and she smacked her lips.

"Don't use my baby against me bitch!" She laughed and I sighed.

"I miss you YaYa. What are you doing?" I asked and she smacked her lips.

"What else you think I'm doing? I'm doing what I do best." She smirked and I laughed.

"Get me and Ashton something." I told her and she smacked her lips again. "Don't play with me hoe!" I said and she laughed.

"Alright bitch. I'll see you in a minute." YaYa said and we hung up.

I dialed Skylar number and it went to voicemail. It had been doing that for a few days now, and I shot her a text "Call me."

I went to the thread from Miles and blocked his number. I know I told Santana to kill Miles but thinking about Ashton growing up without his real father did something to me.

Knock knock knock!

I jumped at the pounding on the front door and grabbed my phone and gun. Santana made sure he told me about all the stashed weapons Mama Mary had around the house. I didn't go nowhere without the gun Santana bought me a few months ago. Soon as I got downstairs, I could hear laughter and talking from the kitchen. Going around the corner,

Amari and her friend was sitting and eating. Amari's friend was holding a small baby.

"Hey sis?" Amari greeted.

"What's up Mari?" I smiled.

"You are not going to introduce me?" the girl said and I smiled.

"We met already at the park. Congratulations on the baby." I said as she rocked a baby in her arms...

"Oh yeah. You was with Santana. Wasn't you?" Amari's friend said then rolled her eyes.

"We were just talking about me having a sip and see... so everyone who missed the baby shower could formally meet my baby girl." She said and I smiled.

"Aw, that's cute." I told her and she laughed.

"Come on. We getting ready to leave anyways." Amari said grabbing her friend's hand. "Deja, chill out!" Amari said lowly.

"Girl. She can come to her step-daughter's shower!" Deja snapped. I swear I hope this fool tell me she was Miles baby momma, hopefully she could get this nigga off me.

"What you mean step-momma?" I wondered.

Santana walked into the kitchen with bags in his hands with Yaya right behind him.

"What it do cuz?" Yaya smirked hugging me.

"Hey baby!" I beamed hugging Yaya.

"I been calling you. I have something important to tell you." Deja said to Santana.

I just stared at their interactions. I have been wondering if this "Deja" that's been calling Santana. I looked at Santana waiting for him to reply but he ignored her and focused his attention on me.

"What's up ma? Y'all ready?" He asked and I smiled.

"Of course. Let me get Ashton ready so he can go with

Yaya." I told him and walked towards the stairs with Yaya on my heels.

"This is nice cuz. I see why you been hiding out here." Yaya complimented.

"Miles been threatening me." I told her once we got in the room. Ashton was sleep still so I went to the closet.

"Did you tell San?" She asked as she sat on the bed.

"No. He has been real busy! I didn't want to bother him right now!" I sighed and looked at YaYa.

My cousin Yasmine was real pretty. She stood at about five six, one-hundred and seventy-five pounds. YaYa has weight all in the right places. She had tattoos everywhere and gold teeth in her mouth. My cousin was the real definition of a bad bitch! She stayed fly and with her hair, nails and everything done! YaYa was four years older than me and could hustle her ass off!

"Tell him now Aja! Miles ain't nothing but bad news! I'm telling you!" She said and smiled. "You glowing. Are you happy?" She asked smirking.

"Happy as hell." I laughed and returned the smile. YaYa shook her head.

"Well you know they put Miles out the apartment so he shacking up with some little chick out east!" She told me and I shrugged.

"Santana been harassing me about moving in with him." I told her and got Ashton bag together. "We are going downtown tomorrow to change his last name. San wants Miles to sign his rights over." I told her giving her the tea on what's been going on lately.

"You okay with that? I love you and San and I think that might be a good idea!" She said and I nodded.

"Yeah that's the move." I told her. I grabbed Ashton out her hands and started to kiss all over him.

Santana walked into the room.

"What's up little man?" He said and Ash reached for San. After we chopped it up for a few more minutes, Yaya got Ashton and they left. I decided to get me some clothes on. After washing and drying my body, I slipped on some pink panties. I pulled some ripped jeans over my body that I got from Fashion Nova and slipped a yellow, red, white and green tube top belly shirt on. Santana came in the room drinking out a bottle of water. He sat on the bed as I slipped my feet into some yellow Converse. My hair was done by me in some thick, curly weave.

"You look gorgeous ma!" He complimented me and I smiled.

"Thanks babe!" I told him and slipped on my bracelets and necklaces.

"I got a few stops then we can go check on Sky." He told me and I nodded. After grabbing my earrings and purse we went on our way.

Chapter Thirteen

SKYLAR

Every since my first mission, I been doing them back to back and the money has been lovely! I don't even feel guilty about the shit I been doing anymore because at the end of the day I'm getting both of what I love most, dick and money. Now don't get me wrong, I don't always have to have sex with them but sometimes I do for the fuck of it.

Right now, some old school owe a powerful man fifty grand. I was here to collect. My father got connected with some powerful ass niggas while being locked down. They protect my dad and pay me to get rid of they dead weight. I wasn't tripping at all. Like I said, the money was great! My dad gave me a target that like to fuck on young girls. Old Man June had a weakness for young girls. My father gave me specific instructions for June but at this point I had my own signature so I was ready for it to be time.

I had a few more hours before I had to head out so I started my bath. My body was sore from working so much.

KNOCK, KNOCK, KNOCK, KNOCK!

. . .

"Who is it now?" I thought to myself as I walked to the door in my panties and bra.

I stopped mid step and grabbed my gun from my purse. It was an instinct to be prepared for anything! I always caught niggas slipping, and I wasn't about to be on the end of the stick. Peeking through the peephole, I swung the door open as I looked at Aja and Braylon.

"Bitch! I know you been seeing us call you!" Braylon yelled storming in with Aja right on her heels.

"Hello to y'all too." I smacked my lips and sat my gun down on the table. "Guys, I have just been really going through some things and I haven't been feeling good-," I tried to say but Aja cut me off.

"Okay, but that doesn't mean cut us off. We haven't heard from you in weeks! We were worried." Aja reasoned, and I sat down across from them with my feet under me.

"Okay, sorry guys. I just need a little me time. I'm really going through some stuff and don't wanna bother y'all with my problems. Plus, my dad been reaching out to me." I said and they both groaned.

I couldn't blame Aja and Braylon for hating my dad. He split all our families up. At first, I had ill feelings towards James too! After the time he sat down with me and we talked about what actually happened, those feelings were gone. Plus, he was my father. He was feeding me at this point. Shit, everybody couldn't bag some rich ass young niggas like Santana and Montana.

"Okay, well we just wanted to make sure you were okay. Just don't ignore us! We won't have to slide on yo ass!" Aja said smirking.

"I'm sorry friend. We can do something later on tonight

or tomorrow. Bray, your birthday is coming up. I have something planned..." I told them and Bray sighed.

"My conditions are worse." She said and I sighed.

"What's been wrong Sis?" I asked concerned.

"It's just been too overwhelming. I miss my momma. Montana knows what's going on with me. Then I think I'm pregnant! I'm moving too fast. I know it," Bray said all in one breath.

"Pregnant?" Aja and I said at the same time.

"Yeah... Two months to be exact! Montana doesn't know so don't fucking tell him." Bray said to Aja and she nodded.

"I won't! I'm not going to tell nobody for real. So have you been taking your medicine?" Aja asked and I nodded.

"Yeah sis. You have to take yo medicine for the sake of you and the baby. You don't wanna hurt yourself or the baby." I told her referring to the time when we were in high school, and Bray had cut her wrist. That fucked all of us up. She vowed to never do it again, and I was hoping she never got to the point where she wanted to kill herself again.

After we talked and I promised to meet them tomorrow for dinner they stood up to leave. They both hugged me and headed to the door.

After locking the door, I went to my hot bath and soaked my body. I was gone get some much-needed rest until it was time for me to head out.

———

I stepped out of my car popping my bubble gum. I was rocking some blue jean booty shorts with a white and black crop top. On my feet was some black Converse Chuck Taylor's. My hair was in a high, messy bun with no make-up. Just lip gloss. I had my crossbody purse on with my gun tucked deep inside. I popped my gum and walked towards the building where June and his old ass friends was posted at.

Soon as I got close, June was the first to start calling out to me. I giggled and kept walking as he cat called me. Whistling and being a pervert, he grabbed my arm.

"Dang baby girl, slow down." He said then pulled me closer to him. "What's yo name?" He asked and I giggled.

"I'm Taylor. What's ya name?" I asked biting my lip.

"I'm June. How old are you?" He asked and I smirked.

"I'm 16." I told him and he whistled.

"Damn, you thick as fuck to be 16. I'm too old for you babygirl." He said and I giggled.

"How old are you?" I asked folding my arms.

"I'm 46." He said and smirked. "That ain't too old for you is it?" He asked and I shook my head no. "Let me take you out." He said and I nodded.

"Take my keys, walk around the back and hit the lock. Wait for me. I'll be back there in like 25 minutes." He said and I nodded. He handed me the keys and I switched off. He went to his friends and I snuck to the back where his car was.

When we pulled up to his crib, I shifted in the seat.

"I thought we was going out?" I asked.

"We are... I'm trying to be alone first. You wanna go in? You smoke?"

"Yeah... I don't smoke though." I giggled and he got out. He came to my door and opened it.

When we got in the house he started kissing all on me. I kept pushing him away but when he reached back and slapped me I fell to the ground.

"You gone let me taste that little pussy." He said and pulled his belt off. Wrapping the belt around my neck he pulled it tighter as he pulled his wrinkled old dick out. I started to panic and started to reach for my purse but he yanked it off me and threw it across the room.

Yanking my shorts down exposing my bare pussy he put his face deep inside inhaling my scent.

"Smell good." He said and licked the inside of my legs. "Taste even better." He said and forced my legs open. I started to kick and fight but the belt around my neck grew tighter. "Stay still." He yelled and positioned himself in between my legs. After one force his dick was deep inside me. Old man June literally had two pumps in him until he pulled out and started nutting on my stomach.

"Be a good girl and go get daddy a rag." He said and pulled the belt off my neck. I hurried and stood up and fixed my clothes. Grabbing my purse, I went to the bathroom and grabbed my gun. Cocking it back. June was sitting on the couch when I walked back to the front room. Before he could even say anything, I had already shot his ass in the head. Walking over to his body, I kicked the shit out of him.

"Bitch ass nigga!" I snapped and walked out of the house. Once I got far away I called an Uber to take me back to the club to get my car. This was my last job. I was done with this shit.

Chapter Fourteen

AJA

As I was leaving Skylar's house feeling relieved that she was okay, I got a gut feeling that something was wrong.

"Something is wrong... I don't feel right." I told Santana and he smirked.

"That's probably my seeds I dropped down in you last night." He said and I laughed.

"No, for real, Santana. Something is not right." I repeated and he looked at me.

"Let me call...." Before Santana could finish, Braylon was calling thru on my phone. When I answered, it was silent but I could hear screaming and pounding in the background.

"What's up, Bray? You good?" I asked but she didn't respond. "Braylon! Hello?" I yelled again but she didn't respond. I hung up and dialed Montana's number, which he didn't answer.

"Babe, call Montana. Bray just called me and I think they're fighting." I told Santana. He nodded and picked his phone up from the cupholder. Both our phones started ringing. YaYa flashed across the screen.

"This him now." Santana said referring to Montana. I nodded and answered for YaYa.

"Hey cuz... How's Ashton?" I started to say.

"We just pulled up to the crib. We went to get some ice cream and stuff. What y'all doing?" She asked.

"Nothing, bout to see what's going on with Braylon. She just called me and didn't say anything." I told her looking at Santana as he held the phone to his ear.

"Aw, okay. We about to go in the house.... WHAT THE FUCK!" YaYa yelled then the phone went silent.

"Yasmine? Hello?" I yelled. The phone hung up and I dialed her back. If it wasn't one thing it was another. I didn't need no shit with YaYa getting ran up while Ash was with her though! For some odd reason, I thought about Miles and goosebumps formed against my body.

"What Montana say?" I asked Santana as I dialed YaYa number back to back.

"He said Braylon tried to kill herself again. It's not looking good for her." Santana said and I sighed. I dialed YaYa and she answered on the first ring.

"Oh God, cuz, he got Ashton! Miles took Ash!" She cried out.

"What? I don't understand! YAYA!? YAYA!?" I continued to yell into the phone and received no response.

"Go to Yaya's babe, NOW!" I told Santana and he quickly U-turned in the middle of the street and headed towards YaYa.

My mind was somewhere else. All I thought about was Miles and the shit he was texting me.

The messages that Miles sent earlier today kept flashing in my head. I started to pray to God that Miles hadn't took my baby. Feeling inside my purse I made sure the gun Santana got me was unlocked and loaded.

"What did she say?" Santana asked me calmly. YaYa's words saying Miles took Ashton kept running through my mind.

"He.... Miles took Ashton, Santana. He took our son."

SUBSCRIBE

Text Shan to 22828 to stay up to date with new releases, sneak peeks, contest, and more....

SUBMISSIONS

To submit your manuscript to Shan Presents, please send the
first three chapters and synopsis to
submissions@shanpresents.com

CPSIA information can be obtained
at www.ICGtesting.com
Printed in the USA
LVHW021500100220
646420LV00003B/463